THE
MISERY
HOUSE

THE MISERY HOUSE

BOOK 1

THE HOUSE ON THE HILL SERIES

DAVID KUMMER

Published by David Kummer

Edited by Marni Macrae
Cover design by Aspire Book Covers
Interior design by Jordon Greene

Printed in the United States of America

FIRST EDITION

Hardcover ISBN 978-1-0879-1878-5
Paperback ISBN 978-1-0880-5936-4

Fiction: Psychological Thrillers
Fiction: Ghosts
Fiction: Small Towns & Rural

This book is dedicated to
my mom, my grandma, and my wife,
who all taught me perseverance
and how to overcome.

The house was said to be abandoned, said to be haunted. And it was both of those things, but it was also more.

Three things happened that year which will never be forgotten in New Haven. First, people started to disappear in peculiar ways. Second, a little boy stood in the rain until he met a guilty stranger driving a truck. And third, the house on the hill had visitors for the first time in many, many years.

PART 1
AWAKENINGS

CHAPTER 1
BENJAMIN "CLIFF" WOODS

From the old, dusty baseball field, it was impossible not to notice the Donnelly house. From our seats in the bleachers, we had a perfect view of the hills. North of New Haven, those unremarkable hills held one remarkable thing: the abandoned house. It waited, looming over us. But by the time it woke up, I'd already gotten used to the view.

I was at the baseball field for Nate's game, like any other weekend. Over the summer, his middle-school team had a game every ten days, but they were blazing hot and sometimes hard to sit through. Even when it was my own son, I had to admit the games weren't thrilling. But the game that day—and all the events after it—were anything but boring.

I didn't see the smoke right away. It rose to our right, from Main Street, a trail of grayish-brown spreading into the blue sky. I was staring straight ahead at the action on the field. While that omen grew with each minute, I'd blocked out everything but the game. A close contest, enough to hold my attention.

Jeremy Adams—a farmer like myself, my oldest friend—noticed the smoke first. He was sitting beside me, without as much interest in the game. He never had any kids to root for or raise. I think he watched our town the same way I watched my children.

Maybe that's why he took the tragedy so seriously from the jump. What happened over on Main that day was just the beginning. Unlike most of us, Jeremy somehow knew. A parent's sixth sense, you might call it.

We were both sitting on those old, rickety bleachers where my dad had spectated years ago. Now it was my turn. My son, Nathaniel, was standing out at second base. I watched intently, focused on the dirt triangle, waiting for the resounding clang of a metal bat against ball.

The opposing team's next batter stepped to the plate. It was the top of the last inning, and this kid from out of town would either take the lead or lose the game. So you understand why we all watched the diamond, the players in their dirt-streaked pants, with so much focus.

Down the row from me and Jeremy, there was a quiet family, a single mother bookended by young children. They were all sitting stiff and silent. She wore a light-colored dress and her children were in khaki shorts and button-ups, which I found odd. Maybe if it'd been Sunday, their church clothes would've made sense.

The mom was as focused on the game as anyone else, so I assumed she had a kid playing but I didn't know which team. I guessed they were from the opposing team, out-of-town, since I'd never seen them before. They were the quietest people in the whole crowd and they stood out like a sore thumb, so I kept my eye on them.

One fellow who was *definitely* from out-of-town—a few rows down from me, one of the opposing fathers—muttered, "If he gets a nice crack at it, game over," and reached for his potato chips. He was a big guy, loud, and he'd spent the whole game living or dying with every pitch, every throw. Spilled half his potato chips yelling at the umpire. That was my first clue he wasn't from around here: Nobody in this town would lose their cool if one singular thing didn't go their way. We knew how to handle adversity.

This man spent the whole game chomping incessantly to his wife, who didn't give a damn. Maybe it was their kid at the plate. I didn't know or care. I'd seen my share of annoying baseball-dads and I savored the opportunity to root against them. I just needed Nathaniel's team — the home team — to come out on top. It would wipe that greasy grin off his face.

"Hey, Cliff..." Jeremy nudged me, using the nickname he'd given me back as friends in grade school. "Look at that, over on Main Street."

I shooed away his hand and leaned forward. The smell of hot dogs and sweaty uniforms rose to meet me. There was dust in the air, a faint cloud of it, kicked up from the baseball field or brought into town by the relentless, east-facing winds. It seemed everyone in the crowd held their breaths, because all I could hear were the coaches jabbering to their players, the concession stand conversations, and the distant sound of sirens.

A runner on third. Two outs. New Haven's middle school team led by one. From my seat, the three most important players were right in a row. The batter (probably that big guy's son), the pitcher, and Nathaniel on second base.

"He's been making plays all game," I said to Jeremy, but mainly to myself. "Just need one more..."

The pitcher threw one, and umpire signaled "ball." I tried to laugh, 'cause it was a bad call, but my stomach had twisted into a knot and I couldn't sit up straight. Instead, I hunched over, gripping my knees, feeling sweat trickle from my shoulders to my underwear. It felt like an eternity between each pitch. Then came the next.

The pitcher wound up and threw. Nathaniel crouched down, glove extended, ready.

"Strike one!" the umpire called. The crowd cheering drowned out Jeremy's voice, as he again prodded my sides. I didn't look over.

I breathed a sigh of relief. Maybe Nathaniel didn't need to make a game-saving play. He'd had his share of good moments throughout the game. In my nightmare, the ball would fly right over his head. Even if I'd pretended not to care for most of the afternoon, like the other parents in the crowd, I lived on every possibility. I would love a stress-free strikeout.

It didn't matter how good Nathaniel had been, how spectacular his throws and base-running. If he made the game-losing play, it would wreck him. It always hurt to see that.

"He's been working hard," I said again to Jeremy. "Looks like a new player..."

Jeremy murmured something beside me, but the second pitch flew and the batter missed with his swing. "Strike two!" the umpire roared, and I clapped enthusiastically. The opposing dad didn't turn around but part of me wished he would.

"Get lost, ump!" he roared, smacking the bleachers with his chip-free hand. "That was way outside!" Other people shouted similar things, but I didn't care, 'cause the call was already made.

This time, Jeremy nudged me hard in the ribs, hissing something that was lost in the crowd noise. I again shooed him away.

"*What*, Jeremy. What is it?" I didn't take my focus off the diamond for even a second. Pitch three was coming any moment.

"Look at that smoke... Is that George's shop?"

I turned just a hair. "What are you talking—?"

A collective gasp as he pitched. It didn't sink as quick as the first. I knew right away it would be a hit. I almost hid my eyes as the play unfolded.

Crack! The violent sound of the bat. That kid really got a hold of it.

"Whoo!" the dad in front of me cheered, rising to his feet. I jumped up and stared, dripping with anxiety.

In unison, the crowd around me also stood. The ball sped off like a bullet, barely missing the pitcher's torso. It whizzed through the air, and my eyes flashed directly to Nathaniel, even before the ball reached him. Everything moved so fast.

He stuck one foot in the ground and leapt into the air. One sweat-slickened arm reaching up, stretching out. His feet were off the ground, his body lurched. With a thud, Nathaniel collapsed to the ground. In his mitt, he clutched the dirty baseball.

"Out!" someone roared. Half of the crowd leapt into the air. I high-fived a few people, noticed the dad in front of me seething. He made a show of stomping the potato chips under his feet. The third-base runner dropped his head and the batter spat on the ground. But nothing gave me the feeling of ecstasy quite like Nathaniel's reaction.

He glanced up, straight at me, and smiled, waving his glove in the air. His eyes were wide, brown skin glistening in the sun, his uniform streaked with dirt. And then his team mobbed him, and I at last turned to Jeremy, beaming wide.

It'd been a good hit. Straight on in a dead heat, almost over his head. But Nathaniel had moved impossibly fast for a middle-schooler. He'd made the play, and I could breathe easy now.

What a rush.

"You see all that?" I asked Jeremy, but my smile quickly fell away.

He was also standing, gazing in the direction of Main Street, where a thick, dark cloud had gathered over one of the buildings. Jeremy's face was ashen, and his bearded jaw had fallen open. Through the gaps between buildings, I could make out a crowd of people and two fire trucks. The smoke continued to billow into the sky, and I wondered how far the flames could spread. If they were contained already, or if the whole block over there was in danger.

"Isn't that George's?" he repeated the question, pointing.

That ball of smoke overwhelmed me now. There weren't any flames visible, not from this far away, but the cloud appeared to be growing, even now. It reached up toward the pure sky and spread over top of Main Street like it wanted to block the sun altogether.

The smoke didn't really matter. I just wanted to know how bad the damage was, if anyone had been injured. But the smoke was an omen of far worse things to come.

"I think so…" I shook my head and felt dizzy, swaying a bit. "Oh, God. That poor guy."

"I'm gonna run over and see what's going on, see if I can help." Jeremy started to descend the bleachers, pushing between strangers and friends. He threw one look back at me, nodding solemnly. "I'll come find you later."

"I'll be at the house," I called, unsure if he'd heard.

Jeremy raced off without another glance or word in my direction. As soon as his heels struck the gravel, he broke into a brisk jog, weaving around the bleachers and back toward Main Street. While I watched him leave, I noticed others were turning in that direction. A handful of men ran to catch up with Jeremy.

New Haven did have a fire department, but they hadn't been tested in years. Nothing ever happened around town, especially not big ass fires in a family-owned shop.

There was an even thicker cloud of dust choking the bleachers now that people were moving about. I watched as the crowd began to disperse. Many of them collected their athletes, hauling the bags and any remaining concessions back to their vehicles. About half would leave town, never to return, and the others would stick around, some of them heading out to farms just like my own. A handful of men and women made straight for the smoke, while others walked toward the opposite end of town. But as I stared at the gaggle dispersing, five minutes later, Nathaniel still hadn't emerged from the dugout.

At this point, there were very few people left standing around, so I lumbered down to the bottom row of the bleachers and sat there, waiting. It smelled different now. There were no food aromas, no heavy-breathing, potato chip-eaters. Just the distant sound of commotion, of sirens. Every few minutes, a yell would resound from Main Street. I tried not to think about what was happening over there.

The coach of the middle-school team — these days, I knew him as "Coach Baggs" from all the stories Nathaniel had told me — headed in my direction. As I huffed to my feet, he said goodbye to the one remaining family. I recognized the single mother with her three children, two of them in church clothes and the oldest in his baseball uniform. The kid hadn't played a single pitch, not as a batter and not in the field. All three of them wore blank expressions and huddled close to her.

But the stranger thing was, I'd never seen that family before. They must've been new to town. In New Haven, we *rarely* had new people, and they didn't stick around long. They didn't usually show up to baseball games.

— When I'd moved back with Naomi and started our family, things went smoothly 'cause I'd grown up here. But a new family altogether? Bold choice.

Coach Baggs prowled closer, still wearing his baseball cap and dirty jeans, complete with his official coaching top, which was basically an oddly designed adult baseball jersey. He was a broad-shouldered man, deeply tan, with the kind of farm-muscle that only Jeremy could match around here. He approached me and stuck out a hand, curling his lip.

"Nate'll be out in just a sec." His grip was rough and firm, like his voice. "That kid'll be a star if he keeps it up, I tell ya."

I smiled and crossed my arms. "He's been working hard, no doubt. He gets all his talent from his mom. I'm no athlete."

In truth, Nathaniel and his sister got a lot from their mom. Appearance, complexion, temperament, skills. It was a good thing, though, because Naomi was radiant, electric, beautiful. Myself… I was boring, bland, and white. Very New Haven.

Coach Baggs eyed me with a mixture of pity and disdain. There was understanding in his eyes. He'd known me for a long time. We both grew up in this backward, middle-of-nowhere town.

Back then, I knew him by a less official name. Our school days were filled with sports, farming, and just a little bit of school. If we weren't helping our dads on our respective farms, we tried out every sport possible, anything to pass the time. Baseball and foball were the most common, played in the evening, while the sun sank behind a distant line of oak trees.

One key difference: he was always the first picked, and I was the last.

But we went through it all together and turned into men.

The past few years, sure, I'd put on some weight — more than

I cared to think about. And my hair had started thinning, both in volume and color. Coach Baggs had somehow maintained his strapping, broad-shouldered, youthful look. He still had a reputation around town as a man with strong fists. I'd become the overweight tractor-driver who worked long hours for little reward.

"Well, I sure am excited to see him develop," the coach said, scratching at his chin. His eyes moved past me to the dramatic scene beyond, hovering over and amongst the buildings. "Say, you know what's going on with that smoke funnel?"

"Not a clue." I jerked my thumb back over my shoulder, toward it—whatever *it* was. "Jeremy ran over."

"S'pose I will too, then."

Before he could budge, I spoke up. "Hey, that family you were talking to. They from around here?"

Coach Baggs looked over toward the parking lot, where they were climbing into a dingy minivan. He chewed on his lip as he watched. "Yeah, their kid's a bit... different. They just moved here a week ago. Last name something like Dawes."

"Different can be good." I paused and scratched my head, turning back to Baggs just as their minivan shifted into gear and rolled away. "You know where they moved into? I didn't think we had many vacant places around here. Decent ones, anyway."

"Couldn't tell ya. Maybe somewhere on Main? I doubt they got a farmhouse." He shrugged, folded his arms. "Strange, though. We ain't had fresh blood here in years."

"That's what I thought."

He smiled at me. "You never counted as fresh blood. Your wife, maybe, but she's, uh... a bit different, right?"

Again with that phrase.

Coach Baggs clasped me on the shoulder—I tried not to

wince—and started to stroll by. His vision flicked to the looming tragedy. "See ya around, Cliff. Keep on Nate for me. He's got real potential. Don't wanna waste it." He offered a wink and then moved on, kicking up dust as he jogged away.

I took a seat on the bleachers again, rubbing the back of my neck. I certainly had never been fresh blood here, he was right about that. But it irked me when people called Naomi "different" in any way. They called her that because of her skin, and because our kids were a shade darker than their own. But she was a hell of a lot more normal than people here.

I loved New Haven; it was my home, always had been. But people tended to think *they* were in the right and not hanging on to some backward way of life. Naomi was perfect in a way they'd never understand.

The ballpark was empty now, except for Nathaniel, who appeared by the dugout and started toward the exit gate. He walked slowly, like he was sore, and smiled quietly to himself.

This baseball diamond, separated from two sets of bleachers by a chain-link fence, had looked the exact same for decades. That dusty infield, the way it clung to his white pants, the far fence where I'd never been able to hit a homerun... This place would always be familiar, nostalgic. Even the scoreboard hadn't changed, not one bit, since I played here. Not that I'd had any success, like Nathaniel. I was a born benchwarmer, part of the background. Felt like sometimes I still was.

Despite growing up in New Haven, despite owning a farm outside of town like so many others—and like I'd dreamed—I never felt exactly right. I didn't have something the rest of the people here did, even back as a kid. When I left for college and met Naomi, it only set me apart even more. She was more beautiful than any woman from New Haven, tougher than all of them. It had been the right choice to start a family here, but not an easy one. At least our kids were taking after her in all the best ways.

Obsolete, I thought to myself as Nathaniel approached, grinning from ear to ear. *That's what I've become.*

"Hey, Dad." Nathaniel sank under the weight of his backpack, with two bats sticking out from the top. His arms and neck were sweaty, caked in dirt, and his dark, curly hair stood wild, unkempt. But his smile was radiant as he held out a baseball, resting on his palm. "Coach Baggs said I could have today's game ball."

"You deserve it." I reached out and ruffled his hair, feeling sweat cling to my hand. "That was a great catch you made."

As I stood from the hard seat, Nathaniel looked past me to the smoke rising over Main Street, but he didn't comment on it. I assumed that he would just push it from his mind, the strange way that kids can. To him, there were more important things to discuss.

"I wanna hit a homerun next game," Nathaniel said, tossing the ball from one hand to the other. "Can we practice later?"

"Maybe... Depends." I turned around now and couldn't tear my eyes away from the smoke as we walked toward the gravel parking lot. My rugged, blue truck waited just ahead. "Let's see what's going on at home, if your mom's feeling any better, and if Jeremy comes looking for me."

"You mean about the fire?" Nathaniel asked. He heaved the backpack off and carried it the rest of the way to the truck. As he tossed it into the bed, he said, "I hope everyone's okay."

"Me too, buddy." I strolled to the driver's side and had just curled my fingers around the door handle when I noticed a man walking in our direction.

He came down one of the smaller side roads branching off

from Main Street, feet moving in a hurried, staccato rhythm. I knew who it was right away from the uniform and the sheriff's hat that his father also wore back when we were both kids. Wheeler had been a hat-guy ever since middle school, but back then it was baseball caps. Now he was almost never out of uniform, never bareheaded. Longtime friends are funny like that. You see them change.

"Sheriff, how's it going?" I called out. I motioned for Nathaniel to climb out of the truck and stand by me. With a slight groan and stretching his shoulders, he did as he was told.

Sheriff Wheeler hurried over, casting looks to either side, as if watching for somebody. Behind him on Main Street, a firetruck roared past and its red frame—sirens screaming through the desolate town—plunged into the cloud of smoke. The street itself was beginning to cloud up, not just the sky, but I assumed things were somewhat under control if the sheriff had come all the way over here. At this point, I figured everybody in town had seen the goings-on, and there were likely a plethora of able-bodied men and women over there to help.

"You all okay?" Sheriff Wheeler asked, hesitating when he saw Nathaniel come around the front of the truck. He studied the boy for a second and then focused on me again. "Where's the girls?"

"Naomi's home, got a bad migraine. And..." I paused, rummaging through my brain. "Not sure about Kaia. She's somewhere in town, safe, but I gotta pick her up on the way home."

"Teenagers, huh?" Sheriff Wheeler didn't smile. His eyes roamed the baseball field, but when he saw nobody left, he locked eyes with me. The man leaned back slightly, sticking out his holster, and shoved both thumbs in his belt loops. "I'm just going around, checking on folks, making sure all's safe." He added, "You seen a new family at the game today?"

I rubbed the back of my neck. "Yeah, I did. Dawes, right? Why, you looking for them?"

"Not particularly. Not yet..." The sheriff frowned at something behind me, then he looked at Nathaniel. "You win today? I bet you're a good player."

"Yeah, we did." He smirked, meeting the sheriff's eyes with no fear. "And I like Smith. That Dawes kid. He's not super smart, but he's really nice."

The sheriff scoffed and raised an eyebrow. Then he looked back at me.

Before he could go on, I asked, "You got all that under control?" I gestured at the smoke, in case he hadn't understood.

He answered without turning around to face it. "Yeah, got it handled. Can't save the store, though. Real shame..." His eyes glazed over and he looked past me again, but I shook him out of it with a question.

"Any idea what started the fire?" I reached for Nathaniel and held his shoulder, though he squirmed out of my grip.

"Still investigating, working on it..." Sheriff Wheeler lost his determined stance and let his shoulders slump. "Poor George." He shook his head.

"That store's been in his family long as I can remember," I said.

"Longer than either of us have been alive," the sheriff added. "Couldn't have happened to a better guy. It ain't right."

I tried not to imagine what the aftermath would look like. I'd been in that store myself so many times over the years, knew the aisle layout back and forth. One of the few places around here that'd sell you a bucket of nails and a toy truck at the same time.

George also had a sweets counter, and he always had the lowest-priced candy in town, like the old days. You could get stuff for a quarter or less. I'd bought it from his dad when I was a kid, and now my kids bought it from George.

I thought to ask, "Anyone inside when it started?"

The sheriff didn't meet my gaze, nor did he respond right away. His eyes flicked to Nathaniel, just for an instant, and they were filled with agony, worry. And then he looked at my battered, blue truck and he stared, unfocused, for a solid ten seconds.

At last, he spoke up again, in a deadpan, defeated voice. "Won't know for a bit. But I... I should be going. Finish my sweep of Main Street. Give me a shout if you hear anything 'bout the Dawes, will you?"

He tipped his hat to me, then turned from us and started back the way he'd come. I looked down at Nathaniel and told him to climb back in the truck. In that same moment, I made the split-second decision to chase after some real answers. The sheriff's response had been noncommittal at best, downright dodgy, and maybe without Nathaniel around he'd give me something more concrete.

"Just a minute," I said to my son, then I jogged to catch up with the other man. It only took a few seconds before I met him, kicking up dust with my toes as I came to a stop. "Sheriff, hey, listen—"

When Sheriff Wheeler turned to me, his face was colorless, forlorn. He cleared his throat and cast his eyes to the heavens, taking a deep breath. Then he touched me on the side of the arm. "I can't tell you much, Cliff."

"Give me something, at least," I persisted. "Stuff like this... this doesn't happen around here. You know that, I know that."

The sheriff sighed and relented. He cast one glance back at the truck, with Nathaniel inside. If you ignored the smoke, the sky above us was crystal clear, not a cloud in sight, though we might've welcomed them. A rainstorm could put out the fire, strengthen my crops. Or maybe it would only make things worse.

And under that endless, blue sky, Sheriff Wheeler said something I'll never forget.

"Something strange is going on, Cliff. Something... not normal. And when I find out who done this..." He started to back away now, though he wasn't finished speaking. "Take your kid home. I'll get back to you later or send Jeremy to fetch you. The three of us... we need to talk."

And with that, he disappeared fully, turning his back before I had a chance to respond. I stood there for a moment, scratching at my beard, biding time before I would return to Nathaniel and drive home. The sheriff had given an answer alright, though it was exactly what I'd feared.

From the moment he glanced at my son with that specific expression, I had suspected it. Whatever started the blaze in George's shop, whatever they decided to do with that storefront rubble, something had changed irrevocably in New Haven.

He would only look at Nathaniel like that for one reason, only keep the truth hidden that long for one thing. Somebody had died. And they might not be the last.

CHAPTER 2
KAIA WOODS

"Girl, you know how my mom is. I've gotta get back to the house to do chores and stuff."

I stood on the sidewalk with the newlywed couple. Malaki's obnoxious, red convertible was parked in the street next to us. He and Allison — now the Banks — were still dressed up, hand-in-hand, oblivious to the heat. Allison wore her low-cut, gorgeous white dress and a beautiful smile. Malaki sported a suit.

The church to our side had emptied out entirely. Not that long ago, it was packed, everybody celebrating. But like everything, the wedding had slowly died off, so now only us three were still around.

"Are you sure you can't come over?" Allison pleaded with me. "Just for a bit, Kaia?"

— Was that fear in her eyes or a reflection from me?

I shook my head and smoothed out the front of my dress. "Sorry, she's texted me twice already. My dad's swingin' by to get me."

I was actually thankful Mom had texted. And I didn't have any "chores" today; I'd lied. But another twenty minutes around Malaki might drive me crazy. Watching him drool over Allison.

I mean, she looked absolutely stunning, but she deserved way more than that asshole.

No, I'd much rather go home, get out of this heat, away from that smoke cloud a few streets away.

"Don't worry, baby." Malaki reached up and slicked back his long hair, squeezing Allison's hand with the other one. "We'll see her later this week. Let's have some alone time."

"I suppose so." Allison stuck out her bottom lip and then giggled. "Kaia, did we tell you our honeymoon plans yet?"

"Nah, don't think so." I listened to them, but my attention was stretched thin as another firetruck wailed in the distance. I saw the flash of red between buildings, heading for the east side of Main Street, the place with smoke hanging over it. Third firetruck, by my count. Not a good sign.

"We're waiting 'til Christmas time," Malaki said. He reached a hand around Allison's waist as he spoke, pulling her closer to him. The two of them took turns describing whatever beachy vacation they'd decided on, but none of it mattered to me.

They were a fine couple, by New Haven standards, but that didn't mean they'd last. Especially when you knew them like I did. Allison and I had been best friends since seventh grade, and I'd been around Malaki for even longer. Much longer than poor Allison. I'd seen the way his eyes would wander.

Back in middle school, he tried to hold my hand once and I'd blatantly refused. (I kicked him *hard* in the shin when he kept trying.) Sure, that's just middle school, but the years stacked up, puberty set in, and Malaki got more aggressive. One day, I had to slap him across the face, right in the middle of a group presentation. The teacher was stunned, the class gaped, and I felt a swell of red-hot pride. That certainly shut him up.

I've never been interested in Malaki. Or any boys in New

Haven, really.

Pretty soon after, he'd turned his sights on Allison. Their families were already friends, and it just made sense they'd end up together. Who was I to stand in the way of fate? On the other hand, who was I to let my best friend get with such an obnoxious dickhead, even if she seemed *genuinely* into him?

Whatever. Too late. Now they were married, and I had to deal with him long term. Hopefully — Kaia to God, hello — Malaki would chill out, like most jerks after high school.

The two of them were done talking and stared at me, waiting for a response.

"Um..." I grasped for something to act like I'd been paying attention. "So, you guys gonna be around for a hot minute, huh?"

"Oh, for sure." Malaki had an arm around Allison still, but his other hand flinched, like it might reach toward *me*.

I drew out my phone to "check the time."

"We aren't going anywhere," he finished.

"Cool, cool." I took a deep breath and stored my phone in my pocket.

One thing my mom taught me is never let a man touch you — not unless you want him to — even if it's something small. And that principle stood opposite to most of my encounters with Malaki Banks.

"I hope those people are okay," Allison said. She was peering in the direction of the smoke, wide-eyed, tears threatening her professionally-done makeup.

Malaki squeezed her tighter and smiled reassuringly. "It'll be okay, honey. Let's head home, don't ya think? Take your mind off things?"

Then Allison was climbing into the passenger seat of his sleek convertible. As he fumbled for his keys and walked to the other side, I bent down and whispered in her ear.

"Babe, hit me up if you need anything, okay? Or if you... just wanna chat?"

Allison nodded, said "Thank you," and even stretched out to hug me, but her features didn't shift. She didn't get what I was *really* saying, my true intent behind those words. Before I could say anything else, Malaki hopped into the driver's seat, not bothering to open the door.

"We better get going." He laughed, turning his key and revving the engine when it came to life. "Damn, listen to her *purr*!"

I rolled my eyes and backed away from the car as he leaned over and whispered something into Allison's ear. She giggled and waved goodbye to me. The convertible lurched into action. I waved back, as it kicked up a small cloud of dirt, obscuring them from view. Malaki whipped out of the parking space, did a wild U-turn into the other lane, and sped away, leaving nothing but dust.

My dad was supposed to swing by in his truck soon, so I walked over to the church steps and took a seat there. At least there was some shade over here. The church's huge steeple and clock tower helped with that.

From those concrete stairs, I could see bits of Main Street between buildings. There weren't many people out, except for the crowd gathered near where the smoke rose. I assumed they had the fire under control by then.

This street was calm. Besides the gray cloud hanging over us, it sat perfectly normal and still; no cops, no fire trucks, nothing but an ordinary, empty sidewalk. Main Street had all the businesses. This one, First Street, had just a church, houses, and some rundown apartment buildings.

The minutes wore on. I found myself worrying for Allison, more than I'd expected to. Seeing her and Malaki drive away felt more real than ever. Even if they weren't going on a honeymoon anytime soon, it was a huge change. It scared me.

That girl, she didn't know how to stand up for herself. And she didn't understand Malaki's flaming hot temper. Even I'd only seen it a few times, but those brief flashes were enough. He wasn't the kind of guy you wanted to be around, or the kind you wanted your best friend to marry. At least I knew how to fend for myself. When you grow up in a town like New Haven with a darker skin tone than everybody else, you've gotta be resilient. You have to be like my mom taught me.

I knew Allison wasn't prepared for all the sarcastic comments and constantly being cut down. Or the verbal abuse he stored like bullets in a gun. I just hoped things wouldn't escalate any further. I really needed to stay in touch with her.

I wasn't saying every guy in New Haven was as terrible as Malaki. But I was nearly nineteen, and there hadn't been a single one that clicked with me. Not that it mattered. I had more important things to focus on. Studying, volunteering, figuring out what to do now I'd graduated high school. I *knew* I was intelligent and gorgeous, and I deserved better than these guys, this town. I knew where I wanted to end up in life. Somewhere way outside of New Haven, at the very least.

Dad's beaten up, blue truck rattled around the corner and brought me back to earth. He spotted me right away and turned on his blinker as the truck drifted toward the sidewalk. Nate scooted closer to him, into the middle seat. I stood from the church steps, flattened my dress, and smiled. After an exhausting day, I couldn't wait to be home. And to be with these people, my family.

"How'd the game go?" I asked as the truck came to a standstill in front of me. The familiar, slightly queasy smell of diesel fumes met my nose. "You kick their butts?"

Through the open window, Dad beamed, one hand resting on the steering wheel and the other touching Nate's head. "This kid played one heck of a game. Made the winning play."

Nate lowered his head and blushed.

I sidled around the front of the truck and climbed in the other side. "You better play like that when I come. You always suck when I'm there."

He narrowed his eyes at me. "Shut up, I do not."

"You know I'm just messing."

I settled in next to the grimy baseball player and buckled my seatbelt. I noticed Nate's two hands were clenched around a dirty baseball, his fingertips gently feeling the grooves and ties. I felt a pang of affection and turned to look out the window as the truck began to move.

That smoke cloud hung over New Haven still, though it didn't seem to be growing anymore. A crowd of people were still gathered around it, though I could only see them through alleyways and between buildings. They formed a sort of stasis with the thick, gray cloud, almost like a funeral. Whatever unfortunate storefront had tangled with catastrophe, it now had an audience. Some of them were standing, others crouched or sitting altogether. I wondered what they were doing, what they could see. But those answers wouldn't come from all the way over here, so I turned straight and gazed out the front window as the town rolled by.

"You wanna tell your sister about the game?" Dad prodded, one hand on the wheel and another draped lazily out the window. His steering wheel had cracks in it and almost as much dirt as the once-white pants next to me.

Nate stared into his own knees and shrugged. I noticed his face was even more red than before and he fidgeted with the baseball. "Um, so... we won..." He glanced at me.

"Yeah, duh," I teased. "What about this 'big play' at the end?"

"The, uh... the last guy hit a line drive. Two outs, runner on third, by the way. It went right past Bobby."

"He's the pitcher, yeah?" I'd picked up a good knowledge of his team 'cause I'd been to *lots* of games. And my mom knew everybody around town, so that sort of filtered down to me.

Nathaniel nodded. He drummed his fingers on top of the dashboard, the baseball now sitting on his lap. "I just jumped and caught it."

"You *flew*," Dad said. He paused and glanced over at a sprawling soybean patch with the sun beginning to sink at its back. *Not as large as my field*, I imagined him thinking. "And you moved awful quick for it."

"I guess so."

I leaned forward a bit to try and get a better view of my brother's face without being too obvious. "That team beat you guys last year, right?"

"Yeah, but... well..." He turned to face me, smirking. "I didn't get to play last year."

"I don't think you'll have to fight for playing time anymore," Dad noted.

The conversation died off as we moved farther into the countryside. I relaxed into my seat and watched the familiar landscape roll by. The fields were lush, mostly beans and corn and others I didn't know. A combine churned through a wheat field, casting a long shadow behind it, kicking up dust clouds.

Everything did around here. Even the wind. I liked to call it dust wind.

Apart from the farmland, there were untouched expanses of land, plains of grass that resisted all tractors and New Haven residents. I loved how the grass would run on, endlessly, and sometimes trees cut between them, like the huge oaks were separating the land into squares on a checkerboard.

There were plenty of forests around here. Deep, dark woods and younger ones. I spent hours and hours out there as a kid, just exploring, trying to find something interesting to do. I would wander off track, have to find my way back home. I would do it still, whenever I had time. Something about the forest makes you feel like a kid. Maybe the size of the trees, maybe the energy. But anyway, the best part of living in New Haven was the wilderness, so much of it to explore.

As the truck rambled on and our home swam into view, I remembered, years ago...

Our house is a good-sized, two-story building with Dad's fields all around. Across the road from us, there's another smaller field, which nobody's using. It's the barrier between worlds. When I was younger, I would tramp through that field in all weather, rock-hard dirt or mud-slush. Whether the grass had frozen and died, making a lifeless carpet, or if it rose above my waist, I would press through. Sometimes Nate came with, once he was old enough.

Either way, I would cross the road, then the field, and enter the forest. Dodging through the first line of trees, I'd stand there, staring into the depths of the woods. Each leaf rustling in the wind like a new adventure awaiting. With Nate, I had to choose easier, less rugged paths. On my own, I got brave, daring it to swallow me whole.

If Nate didn't tag along—or once he got old enough to be trusted—I would wander off to the creek, a little deeper into the trees. After a week of rain, that little stream could turn into a beast, snapping at my ankles and splashing up my pant legs. There was a thick log bridging one section. I could head across that and keep dry, but sometimes I chose to hop down into the stream anyway.

Across the creek, there was an overgrown path leading straight ahead, then curving to the right. It wasn't easy to find unless you knew about it beforehand or had a mom who could tell you. The trees back there were as thick as anywhere else, and the dense vegitation threw off any sense of direction I had (—not much). Like I said, the deep forest made you feel like a kid again.

We spent hours, days, weeks back there, wandering among the massive trunks, canopies overhead like a biodome. Our footprints were covered by decaying leaves and underbrush. But maybe a quarter-mile down that unrecognizable trail lay my great secret. Or at least something great— "secret" might've been exaggerating.

It had taken months, most of a whole summer, but I'd managed to build it all by myself. A small structure. It had a dome-like roof, with shingles, built around a large tree trunk that helped support it. There were a few poles helping to hold it up, and I'd nailed boards across these, making a semi-stable wall on three sides. The front had two more poles, which were dug into the ground, but they didn't obstruct the view. I used only wood, nails, shingles, some large stones... all stuff I carried from the house, with Dad's permission.

That enclosure, with a wooden roof and shingles overtop, had once been nothing. But with my blood, sweat, and tears—mostly just sweat—I turned it into something. After I built the damn thing, I kept some lawn chairs there, so I could chill out. Protected from rain, shielded partially from the wind, I would sit there and enjoy a nice view of the creek bubbling past. Or I'd take a book. Or I'd just listen to the whispering trees and the sing-song harmonies of birds.

The moment I stepped back from it all, wiping dirt off my knees and dropping my hammer, I had grinned like a maniac and spun around a few times. Within an hour, I'd collected Nate from the house and half-yanked him down the trail. The kid clapped and cheered when he saw the finished product, looking up at me with big, admiring eyes.

"What's it called?" he asked, running a hand along the outside.

I stood for a moment, shifting from foot to foot. Then it struck me like a bolt of lightning and I hollered in response. The perfect name. "The Wolf Cave!"

—Look, I was a middle-schooler, and I was into wolves. There are worse names, you know.

A rough bump in the gravel driveway jolted me back to reality. The smell of that old diesel truck and the vinyl seat clinging to my sweaty calves. I took a deep breath and smiled. Dad's truck came to a gradual, crunching stop on the rocks, right in front of the barn. Nathaniel started fidgeting, anxious to get out of the middle seat.

"Home again." Dad tapped on the steering wheel and peered at the front side of the barn. Then he opened the door and hopped out.

"Think Mom made dinner?" Nate asked as they climbed out the driver's side door. Right away, he started rummaging in the bed of the truck for his baseball gear.

"Let's find out," Dad answered.

That barn in front of the truck—Dad's barn—was about average-size for New Haven. He had enough space for a tractor, a few different attachments, and an assortment of animals. (We used to have more, but now it was just the chickens left.) The big, sliding doors on the front were bold red, standing out against our property of mostly greens and yellows. To the side of the barn, a small yard separated it from our home. A typical farmhouse, with a long back porch, two stories, and an attic. But all of its blandness made me feel perfectly at home.

A rectangle of green grass made up our yard. A large oak tree stood alone, behind the house. There was a strawberry patch to its right and a vegetable garden behind the barn. Everywhere else, beyond the grass, had been plowed and planted. There were soybean fields and corn fields, with a section for hay off in the distance.

I knew that around this time of year, all his fields began to buzz with life. It grew from the soil, introducing itself in the hot summer days, pushing higher and thicker into the early fall. I marveled, every year. The passage of time marked by such vivid, changing color palettes. Dirty greens and bright yellows and soft browns and hard reds, cycles dying, reviving. Tiny sprouts growing into full plants, a field full of them, a green ocean. Such simple, beautiful life. —Pretty obvious why I wanted to study Environmental Biology in college.

I stepped down from the truck bench, landed on gravel, and breathed in the fresh, evening air, when the land was finally cooled off and it wasn't an oven outside.

When I saw Nate struggling, I offered a hand. "You need help, kid?"

He heaved the backpack of baseball supplies onto his shoulder and wobbled toward the porch. "I'm okay," he said, voice and back straining.

As his heavy steps crunched to the house, I watched. Mom soon appeared on the back porch, wearing flip-flops. She eagerly called to him about the game, apologizing for the hundredth time that she couldn't go. We had one of those big, wooden backporches as long as the house, like you see all the time in the country. As soon as he reached the stairs, she darted to the bottom, soles flopping against her heels, and hugged him. They stood like that, holding and pulling away, for another moment. Then, together, they dragged the heavy bag up to the porch swing.

"I'm starving," Dad called, coming around the back of the truck to meet me.

Mom rolled her eyes, holding a watering can above one of the flowerpots. There were five of them spread on the wood railing. "Guess you better get to cooking." She winked at me and smiled.

As I opened my mouth to respond, another vehicle started down the gravel road. I heard the crunching sound—tires on rock—before I saw the truck coming, kicking up a white cloud behind it. My dad leaned against his own vehicle, wiping sweat from his forehead.

I stood beside him, gesturing. "Why's Jeremy here?"

He turned to face me, creases deepening. When his eyes met mine, I read him easily. *He's deciding how much to tell me.* No doubt in my mind. But instead of pointing this out, I waited to see what he chose. And then I'd pester him for information if I wanted.

"You saw that smoke in town?" he asked.

"Yeah, 'course I did." I leaned against the truck now, almost copying his pose. There wasn't much distance between us, and I knew Mom and Nate on the porch couldn't hear any of our conversation. "Do they know what happened?"

"No… they don't." Dad tugged at his beard hairs, like he always did when anxious or thinking hard. His vision flicked to the approaching truck, now halfway down the drive, and then up to the porch behind us. "That's why Jeremy's here," he went on. "Supposed to have some answers."

This sounded like an opportunity. I decided not to budge 'til I'd been given some of those answers, so I stayed right there, next to Dad and his truck. We faced the arriving one together. When I looked over my shoulder at the porch, I saw Mom and Nathaniel had disappeared inside, leaving his bag over on the bench swing. So I stood alone with Dad and hoped he wouldn't tell me to head inside.

Might be time to fess up, I thought, narrowing my eyes at him. "I wanna hear what he says."

Dad furrowed his eyebrows and tugged even harder at his chin but didn't say anything. This, I assumed, was permission granted.

Jeremy Adam's red four-door pulled just in front of us. His side windows were tinted, so for a brief moment there were no clues. Then the glass slid down and revealed a red-cheeked man about my dad's age but with frazzled hair and a much bushier, longer beard.

Jeremy Adams was rarely seen without a smile on his face or a twinkle in his eyes. Now he was staring at my father desperately, and his forehead was creased.

"What's the news?" Dad asked, not leaving the side of his truck. He said it loud enough to include me in the conversation, and I made a note to thank him later.

Jeremy didn't hesitate. "Something awful, Cliff." He glanced from my dad to me, shaking his head. "Sheriff's headed to my house. You and me should go now. He wants to talk."

"But what happened?" I said, taking a step closer to the red truck. "Was the fire on purpose?"

I felt both men look at me now, and I wasn't sure why. Had they not thought of that already, or did they just wanna dance around it forever? It only made sense. Either a fire started on accident or on purpose, and there were rarely ever accidents of that size in New Haven. Whatever the case, I stood my ground and waited for a response, from anybody.

"Go on, Jeremy," Dad insisted, though his tone was less forceful. He sometimes annoyed me with how push-over he could be.

"I sure hope it wasn't on purpose," Jeremy continued, rubbing the skin between his eyebrows as if fighting a headache or a bad image. "They found two bodies, Cliff. George was in there, of course... and a kid."

I didn't have to see my dad's face to know how he felt. He jumped into the passenger seat of Jeremy's truck instantly.

Before I could process that horrible news, before I could even really think, the vehicle was out of park and starting to turn away.

Dad shouted, "Tell Mom I'll be back in an hour!" and then they were gone, in a flash of dust and twilight.

CHAPTER 3
BENJAMIN "CLIFF" WOODS

"I never notice it from my house." I gazed up at the hill in the distance. A fly buzzed near my ear and I tried to shrug it off, but the pest remained.

Jeremy sat across from me, leaning back in his chair, feet propped on the table. The burgeoning, rough-edged farmer never looked quite as peaceful as he did on this back porch, blocked from the rest of New Haven by the house and winding roads. Right when we pulled into his driveway, he became a lot more relaxed, seemed more in control. Here, at the back of his house, looking out on a chunk of his farmland, we were separated from everything and everybody else. Only the gentle chirping of crickets and soft rustle of the wind broke our extended silences.

Raising his glass, with a healthy amount of whiskey sloshing around, Jeremy gestured at the abandoned house. We'd been staring at it for the last ten minutes, waiting for Sheriff Wheeler to arrive, but really we'd been watching it our whole lives. The cloud of smoke from earlier didn't hold a candle to this house. It had been hanging over us for decades. Sometimes I couldn't remember if the house was haunted or if it haunted us.

"That place gives me the creeps," Jeremy said, sipping on his liquid courage. — And whenever the sheriff turned up with the full story, I figured we'd both need more of that hard-to-come-by bravery.

I raised an eyebrow at my friend and chuckled. "Why do you live so close to it then? You can't see it this well from my place." I took a gulp from the glass of water in front of me, then placed it back on the table.

"Suppose we all live too close to it." Jeremy's vision was still trained on those decaying walls and overgrown hillside. "Can't ever really escape it."

"You know," I said, "if somebody wanted to burn something, should've taken down that old place. Worthless old shithole."

Jeremy snorted. "I'm sure someone's had the idea. Probably too scared to really do it."

"Yeah, I guess."

"You never know what might follow you back home, you know?" Jeremy shrugged, as if he couldn't care less. "Burn that house, maybe whatever's in there wants to burn yours. I dunno. Seems risky to me."

Our porches were similar, though his wrapped around the whole house. It was sparsely furnished, just a table with chairs around it, along with mechanical parts and farm necessities scattered across random areas. Whenever I let mine clutter up the porch, I had a wife who would keep me in check about it. Jeremy — never one to marry or get into anything serious — littered his porch with tools, buckets, and hardware, among other things.

But from my home, and even from the edge of my bean fields, you could only make out the abandoned house as a distant shape, a towering figure on a faraway hill. You could tell it was classic Gothic architecture, slanted rooftops, tall and oppressive. The windows were like small eyes, miniscule really. On a long, toiling day in the fields, I could block out the sight of it. It blended into the expansive forests and untamed line of hills. It was hidden by the passing tractors and the bustle of New Haven. A thing to remember but not to fear. Not since back then.

Here, on Jeremy's homely back porch, the abandoned shadow stood much closer, even though it was over a mile away. The windows up there were peaceful, like closed eyelids, but with the potential to open at any moment. A cold front door and cracking exterior stared at us, the dark roof and fungus walls only adding to the menace. There were weeds clutching every surface, large shrubs that had outstayed their welcome and outgrown their clothing. It was a wild place, not a civilized one, a house refusing to be tamed. The town had given up trying, and since then it had remained desolate, looming over us.

"You remember going up there as a kid?" I asked him.

I didn't know if he thought about it much, but that event was seared forever in my mind. As I waited for his response, I realized my arms were crossed tight to my body, knees bent, as if clinging to the chair. I tried to relax, loosen up, but the memories were vivid now. They brought a strange mix of odors and feelings to mind. Back then, the sunset had been younger. All the windows were intact. Now, both the house and I lived with shattered glass.

"I sure do." Jeremy coughed aggressively for a moment, taking his feet off the table, and drank more whiskey. He let out a satisfied "ahh" and continued. "After all the creepy stories 'bout that house, I honest-to-God thought we'd stumble on a cult ritual or something! You and me... the only two brave enough to go in, right?"

I nodded, couldn't help but smile just a little. I rubbed at the veins on one hand and sunk chest-deep into memory. "The other boys chickened out. I'd forgotten that..."

There had been four of us that summer evening. Only Jeremy and I had the balls or the stupidity to venture inside. Even *we* only popped into the kitchen area—through a small side-door, not the main entrance. We smelled rotten meat permeating the air, like the worst type of roadkill, got a few seconds' look at the hellhole. Flies were buzzing everywhere. The stench of mold and disease. Just as Jeremy whispered for us to go further, his youthful eyes blazing, we heard it.

Slow, descending footsteps creaking on the stairs, an awful sound. I didn't have the breath to scream. I didn't have the time. Right away, we darted back outside and sprinted, gasping, rolling down the hill we'd climbed. The other two boys were right behind us, begging for details.

After I replayed the story out loud, watching Jeremy's grin widen with each sentence, our eyes met. Each of us took a long drink—water for me—with heels tapping on the wood, a sudden, mutual rush of energy.

"Can't believe we really went in there," Jeremy cackled, fist-pumping with his free hand. "I bet we're the only two dumb enough to ever done it. Not a bad claim to fame, though, you know what I mean? Even if we didn't see any weird cult stuff."

I didn't answer, just took another sip of water, letting my eyes wander back to the hill and its magnetic pull. I didn't want to burst Jeremy's bubble, and it wasn't my secret to tell anyway, but somebody else *had* been inside those walls. And for much longer than us.

Naomi had told me all about her encounter in that abandoned house, about the horrors it held inside. Not "weird cult stuff." Something far worse. She'd done it shortly after we'd moved here. But she'd waited a year to tell me. By then, we were married. Ever since her tears and those chills seeped into my shirt, I no longer wished Jeremy and I had gone into the next room. I didn't even feel that proud of the expedition. Just lucky. Wildly lucky.

Jeremy yawned, drowning out the crickets for a moment, and re-planted his heels on the tabletop. "Wheeler better hurry his ass over here. I've gotta be up—"

"With the sun," I finished for him, smirking. "You need new sayings."

"Nah, that's the point, pal."

The Wheeler family had been in New Haven for longer than either of us, even Jeremy, whose grandpa owned this farmland before he did. Sheriff Wheeler came from a long line of important town figures. His long-gone relative had founded New Haven. Not all of them had been lawmen, but plenty. The whole lineage awfully controlling over this town. One of them—maybe his great grandpa—had been involved with the Donnellys back when they owned the house and an incredible fortune. Maybe the bloodlines crossed over somewhere. I just knew Sheriff Wheeler considered it his duty to protect the town, his birthright.

"You think the sheriff's ever been in that house?" I asked Jeremy, scratching my chin.

"Hmm…" He mulled this over, shaking his glass so the ice gently tapped the sides. "I doubt it. He's probably scared of it."

We shared a laugh at that.

"Yeah, I guess you're right."

The sound of boots broke our discussion. A deep throat-clearing and an unmistakable voice preceded Sheriff Wheeler around the corner of the house. When he saw the two of us, already paying homage to the dwindling sunlight, the man didn't grin or raise his hand. He simply hunched his way to us, head bowed, and took up a third chair at the same table.

"Fellas," he mumbled, gaze still downcast.

"Whiskey?" Jeremy offered, shaking his glass and rattling the ice again. "I've got half-a bottle and glasses inside."

"No thank ya." Sheriff Wheeler placed his hat on the table and scratched at his balding head, even worse off than mine. "I can't stay long. I do got a favor to ask, though."

Nobody spoke for a minute. The sun had nearly disappeared now, setting fire to the world around us, the distant horizon. Every patch of sky burst with color, shades of yellow and orange interspersed with red-hued clouds. They were gorgeous brush strokes and color palettes, reminding you how small everything is, but soon it would fade to night.

"So, you found two bodies?" I prodded the sheriff, trying to get the ball rolling. Propping my elbows on the cold surface next to my drink, I added, "A kid."

Sheriff Wheeler nodded, staring straight ahead into the empty field. His eyes acknowledged neither of us, nor did they register the only visible house around. Instead, they were planted with the crops. I suspected he was imagining his own kid, one young boy, who everybody knew he was extremely protective of. But then again, was I any different?

"George's son." The sheriff swallowed hard. "Right next to him. We… I think, maybe, they were holding each other." A visible shiver ran down the man's spine. I guessed I'd been right about his thoughts.

Jeremy fidgeted in his seat, glancing at the hatless sheriff. "Tell him about the dog," he insisted, eyes flicking to me for a second. "George's dog."

I raised my eyebrows but didn't have to wait long for an explanation.

"The... their family dog went missing about a week ago," Sheriff Wheeler explained, brandishing a hand through the air. His voice was emotionless. "They had signs up everywhere. Dunno if you saw 'em."

"What's it got to do with... the fire?" I looked from one man to the other and back again.

"Most likely nothing."

Jeremy cut in. "But it might, I —"

"He's full of theories." Sheriff Wheeler focused his attention on me now, turning his cheek to Jeremy. "I don't understand what's going on either, but I do know it's reason for concern. You've got kids, Cliff. You know... how it can be. They go wandering, maybe they're looking for a lost dog, and in *that* way, it could be connected, you see? But could be... nothing. More likely they made friends with the wrong kid, and it... cost 'em."

"I still don't really understand."

I hoped I didn't look too confused, but I certainly felt it. The two of them were throwing out strands of information, even warnings, with no coherent centerpiece. None of it connected. It sounded like the ramblings of two, terrified men. Without giving them a chance to pile on more complications, I went on.

"Do you think it was... intentional or something?" I raised an eyebrow at Jeremy. "Do *you* think someone took the dog? What the hell are you two implying? 'Cause it's not making sense."

Sheriff Wheeler stood from the table all of a sudden, catching us both off guard. Jeremy sat rigid in his chair, both feet on the ground. Even though he now towered over us, the sheriff didn't appear angry. Rather defeated, or maybe dejected. And his tone of voice matched the forlorn expression he wore.

"I just don't know, boys," he started. "Listen, I come to you two 'cause you two got roots here. You know what it's like, how this town *operates.*"

He put a strange emphasis on the last word. I exchanged looks with Jeremy, but the sheriff went on.

"Ya seen any new folks around here?" He directed his gaze at me when he asked.

I hesitated. "There's a new family at church, my wife said. The kid's on Nate's baseball team."

"That boy ain't ever gonna play," Sheriff Wheeler grumbled. He scanned my face and then Jeremy's. "Seen anything else weird? Anything unnatural?"

Jeremy snickered. "You mean like my two goats going missing? I told you, Sheriff, that house's got something to do with it."

The sheriff barely acknowledged Jeremy's response. I thought he wasn't going to answer at all, but then he mumbled, "Don't get started with that Halloween shit, Jeremy."

"Hey, you asked." Jeremy kicked back and took another sip of his drink, chuckling to himself.

"So, what do you want from us, Sheriff?" I finally asked. He seemed reluctant to get to his main point, and I didn't want to sit here all night, so I prodded further. "You mentioned a favor."

"Oh, yes. Right." The sheriff cleared his throat. "Well, like I said, you two got roots here. I can trust you. I just need to know, well, if you see anything unnatural. Any strangers doing strange things. Anything off." He nodded at me. "That new family. 'Specially the teenage kid. Just... keep an eye on 'em."

"That's it?" Jeremy asked.

The sheriff shot him a look. "Two of you know we ain't had anything like this for... decades, really." He picked up his hat from the table, losing himself in the star emblem on it, then placed it on his sweat-slickened temple. "All I can say is this, and listen well—New Haven don't get any problems unless we bring 'em in ourselves. We been fine for years, and we will be again, as long as we stay *alert* and keep wary of strangers."

I spoke up. "Strangers? Why?" My mind jumped to the Dawes family at the baseball game. Maybe I was wrong, but it seemed highly unlikely they had anything to do with this fire. Not unlikely, impossible. They weren't the right sort of people. They hadn't even been in town for more than a week.

"You haven't seen that kid." The sheriff glared at me with a heat I hadn't seen before. "Walking around with his headphones, mumbling to himself... I don't like it. Don't like the timing."

Jeremy waved a hand through the air. He was definitely tipsy, as his words started to slur. "Come, now, get offa their back. Why you so bent outta shape, buddy?"

The sheriff growled, "Because strangers mean trouble. New people mean trouble." Sheriff Wheeler tipped his hat to the two of us and stepped back from the table. "And as long as I'm carrying a gun 'round here, we won't be having any more trouble. Not from nobody. 'Specially not some teenage firebug."

Jeremy and I watched him go without a word. As soon as the sheriff disappeared around the corner, we listened for the sound of his patrol car. The engine sputtered to life and faded away, traveling back to the country road and likely into town once more. I wondered if he'd visit George's storefront one last time, if it would even be recognizable or simply a blemish on Main.

New Haven certainly hadn't seen anything like this in decades, but I'd been thinking since the baseball game, and I suspected they were overreacting. A death was a terrible thing, but accidents did happen. And this was certainly just an accident.

We should be careful, and try to prevent another one, but there was no reason to freak out. Definitely no reason to go looking for people to blame.

"He might be a bit nuts," Jeremy chomped on his ice, now holding an empty glass upside down. He stared at it, frowning. "Suppose I am, too."

"You don't seriously think the dog matters in this, do you?" I asked the question, unsure whether to chuckle or not, and studied his reaction.

Jeremy shrugged. "I dunno. My goats are missing too."

"He seems obsessed with this new family in town, the Dawes." I crossed my arms and rolled my eyes, trying to make it *very* obvious how I felt. "I think he's just turning into a stubborn old man. Doesn't trust anybody anymore, unless he's known 'em for years. I'm just glad he never acted like that toward Naomi."

Jeremy avoided my gaze. "Dawes, huh? Never heard of them."

"Single mom, three kids, oldest one plays baseball," I said. "They were right down the row from us."

"I was looking at the fire, unlike *you*." Jeremy sighed and it morphed into a yawn. Then he focused on me, eyebrows furrowed. His eyes were cloudy. "Wanna know what I really think 'bout this whole thing?"

"Go for it."

He pointed one finger lazily at the house towering in the distance. The sunset had given it the illusion of fire, like the old house itself was being eaten alive by an inferno. Maybe it would be ashes one day, but for now it stood, proudly, amongst the flames.

Angry, I thought. *It looks angry.*

"We ain't had any problems with that thing in a while, you

know?" Jeremy bit his lip. His face had turned a shade paler and his hand was shaking. He stopped pointing and let it drop. "Just feels like... Well, y'know. The old stories, 'bout a cult gathering up there. And the dog goin' missing..."

"I don't think they're related," I assured him, though Jeremy's demeanor didn't change.

"Sure, sure. But it... it just feels..." Jeremy shook his head, smacked his forehead once. "I have this worry that fire wasn't everything. Like it ain't over yet. And I think that..." —he gestured at the far-away house but refused to meet its invasive gaze— "I think something like this, it's coming from up there. Somehow..."

My eyes and imagination traveled to the house, on fire in the sky and in my head. I didn't know what "it" was, whether Jeremy meant the house itself or whatever might lurk in its countless shadows. An abandoned house that I suspected might not be so empty. But nevertheless, I did understand the trembling, the anxiety. The urge to keep quiet for fear that it might hear you. Might even see you.

"Maybe you're right," I concurred, rubbing my head. "But I sure hope not."

CHAPTER 4
NATHANIEL WOODS

It was two days after my baseball game, and it was the first time since that day we'd all been at dinner together. —No, three days, because I had practice earlier that day. In the summers, our team only played a game about every two weeks, but we still had practice four times a week.

Our kitchen's right inside the house if you went through on the back porch. We had a table just big enough for us (but it expanded for when our grandparents used to come visit). There was a counter area right when you walked in the door, a microwave and sink to the left with other stuff, and then the table to the right.

Everyone—me, Kaia, and our parents—was in the kitchen, seated around the table. Mom had set out the turkey, green beans, corn, and mac and cheese half an hour earlier. She didn't let us start eating for twenty minutes though, so we were just getting into it. I was pretty hungry from practice, but I didn't eat the mac and cheese because it was the kind that has crust on the top.

I'd eaten two plates already, I think, because I always eat the fastest. (I also run the fastest.) Dad, sitting across from me, was too busy talking to eat quick, and Kaia and Mom on either side of me were right there with him. —They always ate slow, I guess because they didn't have an Xbox upstairs to get back to.

"The corn yield looks pretty good, if I'm guessin'." Dad shoveled a spoonful of that weird mac and cheese into his mouth and said, "We'll be having corn every dinner 'til Christmas!"

"Don't talk with your mouth full, Dad," I pointed out.

He smiled. I went back to eating, as quickly as possible.

"And don't even get started on your *yields*," Mom snapped. "Not over dinner. Nobody cares, Cliff."

"Hey, now." With a sly grin, he took a sip of his iced tea. "That's the first time today. Gimme a break."

Mom had the same expression. I felt her kick him under the table lightly.

Kaia groaned beside me. "Please don't flirt with each other. I don't need that." She stared across the table at Mom and continued with her cob, holding it by the edges.

"You're eating dinner *I* made. I'll do what I want." Mom raised her eyebrows, but I knew she was just pretending to be serious. The three of them were always doing that sort of thing.

"And *I* grew."

"Shut it, Ben." Mom laughed out loud and Dad tried to hold back a smile.

Kaia started talking about the wedding she'd been at, for two people I didn't even know. Well, I knew Allison was in Kaia's grade and they graduated together, but I was too young to remember when the guy went there. Her and Mom were going on about the wedding for the whole time I ate my turkey and corn. I think Dad started to get tired of it, too, but he kept trying to butt in.

"You two feed the chickens today?" he asked at one point.

I tried to ignore this and I hoped Mom and Kaia would too.

"Nate and I take turns now," Kaia said instead. "It's his day."

Dang it.

Dad fixed his eyes on me. "You better not be playing that Xbox if your chores aren't done."

"No, I wasn't." I started shoveling the green beans into my mouth twice as fast.

"Just get 'em after dinner," he said.

"Okay, I will." No reason to eat quickly then. I might even take another helping of turkey and corn.

Kaia had scraped her plate clean too, but she didn't ask to get up and leave like usual. Instead, she pushed back her chair and went to fill her glass with water from the fridge.

"What do you all think about driving into town this week? Maybe go to the movies?" Mom suggested.

She meant driving to a real town, thirty minutes away, where they actually had stuff. A movie theater, a mall, an arcade, and so many restaurants. But New Haven still had a better baseball field, 'cause ours had character and history, unlike the one in town where we played those rich snobs.

I glanced over at Kaia and answered, "Obviously yes."

"Are there even any good movies out?" Kaia groaned.

I asked, "Does it *matter*?"

She rolled her eyes at me. "What about the mall, Mom?"

But Dad interrupted her. "Me and your mom went to the movies one time." He set his glass on the table with a dramatic thud.

"Cliff, the coaster," Mom snapped, pointing at his glass, which was on the bare wooden table.

"This was before we had you, Kaia. When we went," he carried on, smoothly sliding a coaster under his glass, "there was nobody else there—"

"Ew, please don't," Kaia said, taking a seat in her chair again.

"No, no, it's not that kind of story," Dad huffed. Him and my mom locked eyes, grinned, and Kaia let out another groan. "Anyway, this was the 90s, remember."

"The 80s," Mom corrected him. "Don't act like you're still young."

"Anyway..." He went on. "We snuck up to the room where the camera was and talked to the dude in charge of it. And then we came back to New Haven, and this was New Haven in the 80s—"

"So the exact same," Mom cut in, chuckling.

"Well, yeah, but like different clothes and the cars were different. But this was October, okay, so they had this huge, haunted cornfield over where... well, you don't know the guy, but it's a farmer over there—"

"Who isn't?" Mom again.

"You wanna tell the story?"

Kaia joked, "Is there even a point to this story?"

"Yes, there is. So we went to the haunted cornfield, and you know, there's guys with chainsaws or big monsters that'll chase you. Have you all even been to one? Sorry, anyway, this one actor—do you call them actors?—dressed up as an old guy with a chainsaw because he thought it'd be funny. So he runs out and scares us, and it's *the same guy.*" He looked at me and Kaia, smiling wide.

"Wow." Kaia shook her head.

"Okay, well, I thought it was pretty cool." Dad shrugged and finished the rest of his corncob in one motion. "Weird coincidence, huh? Ah, whatever." He stood up from the table, holding his empty glass. "You kids don't understand what it was like back then."

"Oh, yeah?" Kaia crossed her arms. "At least we have phones."

"We had a... cord phone," Dad faltered.

Mom shrugged, crossing her own arms. "Didn't need one."

This conversation—every time they repeated it—put me in an awkward situation. They still hadn't let me get a phone, and I didn't feel *quite* sure that they ever would. But I didn't wanna bring it up again, because they were starting to get annoyed whenever I asked.

Mom went on wistfully. "We didn't even want phones. We were all just... tuned in to the present." I didn't know what she meant or why she said it with that weird voice, but thankfully it changed the subject.

"Yeah, when you're living with a bunch of hippies in flower vans," Kaia smirked. "That's really 'far out,' Mom."

"Don't you start mocking." My mom held up her finger with a stern expression. "I know you're jealous of it."

Kaia's face turned a little red.

Dad got up from his seat, gesturing with a bare corncob. "Hottest hippie I ever knew."

"Oh, shut up, Ben." Mom shot him a side-eye and a grin.

Kaia seemed unimpressed and stood from the table, holding her empty plate. "Your story still sucks, Dad."

He shrugged, "Yeah, true," and reached for his plate.

"The night *did* get more exciting later on," Mom cut in before she could say anything. "But you two aren't allowed to hear about that part." She reached over and smacked my dad's butt as she said it.

"Okay, no, no." Kaia retreated toward the sink, laughing and shaking her head, full blushing now. "You guys are the worst."

My dad laughed quietly, rubbing his head. He and Mom

shared a kiss as she moved around him, grabbing his plate and her own. Then Dad's eyes shifted to me, eyebrows raised.

"How about taking care of those chickens now?" He reached for my plate, since she'd taken his. "I'll wash this for you."

"Alright, deal." I huffed and handed him the dish. My shoes were waiting by the backdoor. I grabbed a flashlight from the cabinet and then I was off into the nighttime.

<> <> <>

To get to Dad's barn from the house, I just had to cross the gravel and go in through a side-door. The chickens had an area inside the barn, one with a lot of hay tossed on the ground and flies buzzing. There was a small gate leading to an outside, fenced-in section of grass. When I strolled over, waving my flashlight around, I was shocked. Two of the chickens, for some reason, were in that outside section.

"Hey, why are you guys still out?" My mom or dad *always* put the chickens up, usually before dinner, even. And definitely before nine PM.

Whatever. Maybe it was the one day they'd forgotten. I let myself into the barn through the side door and stepped through the chicken coop. The smells of chicken poop, feed, and the old barn all mixed together. I didn't breathe too deeply while I moved outside, into the grass area. The chickens inside were all squawking at me, like they were very offended. The two left outside strutted around, bobbing their necks. I shone my flashlight straight on them, and they clucked at me in response.

"Come on, get inside." I started wrangling them in that direction, stomping behind them, whatever I could to get them moving. Once they'd reluctantly moved into the coop, I shut the sliding door separating them from the outside.

The smells got more intense with the door shut. I coughed a few times, searching for the feed bag with my flashlight. Once I found it, I gave them a couple scoops (there's a big, dirt-coated cup in there) and finally left the barn. The chickens were mouthing off behind me, but they sounded happier, now.

"Back to the Xbox," I said to myself.

I left the building and shut the side door carefully behind me. The fresh nighttime air met me, and I took a grateful, deep breath of it. No more gross animal smells. I don't really think I'm cut out for farm life, nothing more than feeding the chickens every other day, anyway.

Strolling over the gravel, that familiar crunching under my tennis shoes, I didn't have a care in the world. All my worries and chores were done with.

Then I heard it.

Something like footsteps, the same crunching noise over gravel. But coming from my left.

I stopped in place. So did the other noise. I shifted, pointing my flashlight at the backside of the barn. The roof stuck out over the two open spaces where my dad would leave his tractor equipment or his hay trailer. I paused, straining my eyes. Nothing seemed unusual. My pale light cast weird shadows on everything.

Maybe I'd heard a small animal over there. Nothing dangerous.

I turned back to the house, crunching along. A moment later, I heard it again, behind me. I was almost in sight of the back porch now, but my heart started racing. I froze and turned again, holding the light up.

Was that a new shadow, leaning against the wall? Right beside the hay trailer. I focused my light on it. The shadow disappeared. Or maybe it wasn't ever there.

Taking deep breaths, I made the decision to not investigate any further. I jerked around and raced for the back porch. Over my heavy breathing and footsteps, I didn't hear any strange noises this time.

When I got to the back door, I waited a moment for my breathing to calm down. I didn't want my parents thinking I was a scared little kid. And it was probably nothing out there, a trick of the light or a small animal. Nothing.

Stepping inside, I tossed my shoes to the side of the door. My heart still beat uncomfortably fast. I put on a fake smile and stretched my shoulders.

Mom and Dad were by the sink, finishing the dishes. He held the towel in his hands and dried each dish as she handed it to him. I heard her say, "...wouldn't hurt anyone, just because he's not like everyone else. That's a stupid—"

She cut off when I entered. Without breaking her scrubbing motion, Mom turned to me and asked, "Hey, there. How'd practice go today?"

"It was good." I almost walked straight out of the kitchen, imagining—back through the short hallway, up the stairs, and right inside my room's door—my Xbox setup. But instead I hesitated by the table and decided to ask something. "At... most kids were talking about the fire. What happened with all that?"

I noticed Dad tense up, but Mom handed him the plate she'd been holding and turned to face me.

"They're not really sure, Nate," she said, frowning. "It's awful, but it seems like it was just an accident." She paused. "Did you know Mr. George?"

"No. And his son doesn't go to our school. Or didn't." I shook my head. "Were you guys talking about Smith?"

Dad's face gave it away, but Mom responded in a soft voice. "We were. You aren't being mean to him, are you?"

"No, I like Smith. He's really nice."

She nodded, offering a warm smile. "Does he... do well in practice?"

I shrugged, leaning against one of the chairs. "He tries hard, but I don't think he's gonna get to play this year. He doesn't run very well."

"Nothing wrong with that," Dad added. He was carrying a stack of plates to the right-side cabinet.

"Just make sure you're kind to him, Nate. He doesn't... He's not like everyone else, so he really could use you as a friend." Mom smiled at me again, but her face was still scrunched up with worry. "Do you wanna bike tomorrow? We haven't been since before your game."

"Um... sure." I glanced between the two of them and tried to muster my most convincing worn-out voice. "I'm pretty tired from practice. I'm gonna go play Xbox... since I haven't all day."

Mom chuckled knowingly and nodded.

CHAPTER 5
NAOMI WOODS

We were almost nine miles into our bike ride when things took a turn for the worse. More importantly, Nathaniel and I were over eight miles away from the house. As day turned into night, the dark tree line on either side of us opened their jaws.

"Feels great out here," I said, glancing over to the side. I continued to push hard, pressing my tennis shoes against the pedals.

Nathaniel gripped the handlebars, his shoulders relaxed as he surveyed the landscape. He grinned. "Sure does. I'm not even tired. What mile are we on?"

We had just crested one of the larger hills and could see for miles and miles in any direction. This stretch of hills, to the north of New Haven, was our favorite biking route. The inclines were challenging but not too difficult, and the views were unmatched. On such a gorgeous evening, the farmlands sprawled out under us, the sky overhead a work of art. If I was any sort of artist, I would've painted it. But it made a perfect environment for such a long bike ride, too. Cool breezes on either side, earthy smells rising from the dirt. In that moment, I felt an intense connection with everything around us, with the wind and swirling clouds and complex leaf arrangements. I couldn't have been happier.

"Over eight," I answered him, checking the fitness watch on my wrist. "We can go a bit longer then turn back. That'll get us to almost twenty."

My son gave a thumbs up and then held on with two hands as we descended the other side of the hill. A wide smile spread across his face, and I watched him soar down the road, a little bit ahead of me. There had been remarkably few cars today, only a handful, and it felt like this entire place belonged to just the two of us.

It was always just the two of us anytime we rode. Nathaniel used it as a workout, strengthening his legs and lungs, improving his stamina for baseball season. I preferred a more leisurely ride, and it worked better than anything else to help me stay in shape. Since I'd taken up biking a few years ago, my body felt so much better, looked better, and my mind had never been so clear. Each time I returned to the house, my legs were aching and sore, but that only strengthened my will to go out again. An hour or two in the countryside, under a dazzling sunset of deep blues and faded yellows, could do wonders for a person. Nothing quite like fresh air, sweet flowers, and exertion.

I invited Cliff almost every time, telling him all about the benefits, but he never tagged along. Despite my constant nagging, even if I went by myself, he would stay at home. Occasionally, he'd draw me a bath or massage my legs after, probably to make up for saying no, but I wished he'd just come along in the first place. He'd complained about gaining weight, but anytime I asked about a bike ride, he found an excuse. Or he said he was "too tired." I didn't feel angry at him, just irritated, and maybe a bit hurt. I wanted to share this experience with him, the sights and sounds of New Haven from the vantage point of birds. Nathaniel's company made up for it, though, and served as motivation. We usually only did ten or fifteen miles on these long rides, but he would push me. Must be nice to be that young and full of energy.

And so, we pushed onward, up the next incline, calves aching and thighs on fire.

"Look at that," Nathaniel called to me, pointing ahead of us. He slowed down at the top of the hill and let me catch up. "There, Mom."

I reached his side and saw it at once. A little way ahead, a single deer stood by the road, in the shadow of the trees. The doe spotted us and watched, not moving, as we rolled along on the other side. With a white-spotted back and a bushy tail, it stood rigidly stiff. Other than the bike tires, there were no sounds, except those of crickets and wind tickling the tree canopies.

"Beautiful..." I didn't look away from it, coasting slower on the bike than at any point so far. Nathaniel didn't try to hurry us along. In fact, he looked just as entranced by the animal as me.

"It's so close to us," he whispered.

The doe moved its head slightly, bent lower, but it didn't bolt away into the underbrush. I peered into its tiny orbs, imagined running my hand along its head and soft, reddish fur. The deer still didn't move as we passed by. It stood with its spotted back to a glistening tree line, the sunset casting strange shadows and vibrant colors, so that all of it became glorious. As we finally moved along, I wondered if it might stick around long enough for us to see it again.

"Watch out, Mom," Nathaniel said, laughing. "We're going down again."

I turned straight ahead and chuckled. He was right. In just a moment, we were speeding to the bottom of the hill, the constant roller-coaster of this terrain. To my left, I could make out Main Street and the surrounding buildings, all of it down below us now. The winding road that led out of town and into the distance, the fields surrounding New Haven, a smorgasbord of crops and tractors. I marveled at how much higher we were, how I could see the flat lands spreading out forever, a checkerboard of forests and farms, creek beds and dirt plains. What a magical place I'd lucked into loving.

—I'd never been a city-person. Before college, where I met Cliff, I had spent my whole life traveling the country or living in a commune down south. My parents were proud hippies, and I suppose I picked up a few things from them. More than anything, I loved the outdoors, and I needed a place with access to that to raise a family. Like New Haven.

The fresh, clean air struck me and it felt like I was flying. Tires picking up speed, passing Nathaniel even, I leaned forward on the seat. The bike plunged to the deepest point of the road. There were hills on three sides, a sharp drop on the left, New Haven past it. Soft, vibrant hues in the sky stretched for eternity. The world smelled of earth and clouds and footprints on the edge of a field. It was made of serenity and sunlight on a country road, peaceful darkness, the cycle of colors. And I wanted to burst with joy, to sing and dance.

When I started to ascend the next hill, with Nathaniel a solid twenty yards behind me, I clutched the brakes hard and came to a screeching halt. *Goddamn it. How did I forget?* We didn't usually come this far, and I guess I just… got caught up in the ride.

My eyes were cast upward, to the top of that hill I'd almost climbed in ignorance. As soon as the bike stopped, my legs ached worse than ever. I hadn't been still for nearly an hour, and now my body didn't want to start again. But none of that mattered, because this was no place to stop and stare. We had to head back, right now. Away from the shadow.

"Damn it, damn it, damn it." I kicked at the asphalt and started to turn my bike around. Huffing and heaving, with my back to that foreboding structure, I felt a little better. But I wouldn't feel safe until we were miles away.

"What's up, Mom?" Nathaniel brought his bike to a halt beside me. He looked from me to the house on the hill, then back again. He raised his eyebrows.

"Let's head back," I said, straddling my bike and starting to walk it back the way we'd come. I didn't want to turn around or even think about that place. "Nate, it's getting dark, so... we should —"

"*Come on.*" Nathaniel rolled his eyes and sat there with his arms crossed. "Let's just... get a little closer."

I looked at him and a shudder overtook my body. He stood, ogling up at the house, a foreboding backdrop perfectly in line. The old structure itself glared at us in front of a fading sunset. It stood against that mesmerizing scene like a hole in the sky. But I knew Nathaniel didn't see it the same way. He stared at it longingly, full of mischief and adventure, the way I once had. Youthfulness. Invincibility. But when it comes down to it, the house shatters every false notion.

"We need to head back," I snapped, unable to move closer because of the bike between my legs. I narrowed my eyes, tried to bite my tongue, but there were emotions and fears bubbling inside that hadn't come out for a long time. Bile rising, a clenched hand around my throat. "Let's go, Nathaniel."

He continued to protest, whining now, still refusing to move. "But I wanna see it closer —"

"I said no!" I started to wheel my bike up the large hill,

toward the friendly deer. Maybe it had waited. Maybe Nathaniel would follow. God, I hoped so.

He kept on grumbling. "I'll go by myself, then."

I whipped around and saw him walking his own bike up the opposite hill. He'd only gone a few steps, but it was enough to make me lose control. Maybe he wasn't gonna go all the way, but I couldn't take that chance.

The sight of him approaching. The images that gnawed at me.

"Get your ass back here *right* now, Nathaniel!" I screeched, jumping off my bike and kicking it to the ground. Over the clattering it made, I went on, my voice angrier than I wanted. But I meant it. "I said no, damn it! I swear to God, if you go any closer, I'm taking your Xbox and TV and I'll..."

Nathaniel didn't say another word. He stared at me for a moment, the two of us locked in a game of silence, of regret. My own tongue locked in place, the air shimmering with rage and anxiety, on the edge of saying things I couldn't take back. As I tried to hold it in, I recognized he'd been stunned into his own silence. The face of my son looked back with confusion, worry. I could almost picture the wound in his chest. I could hear the shredding words he wanted to shout at me.

Nathaniel coasted down the small incline he'd gone up and then started pedaling as quickly as possible. He blew past me and raced to the top of the less dangerous hill before I could say anything, before I could fully study his face. But those knuckles were pale and he moved with a fury I hadn't seen before.

As he distanced himself from me and vanished over the hilltop, I trudged up it myself, moving awkwardly with the bike at my side. All energy or momentum had deserted me—no way I could ride up this hill, so instead I inched along, straining against gravity and the urge to look back. Nathaniel would probably wait for me at the top of this hill or the next one. We would be fine, once I apologized and he forgave me, and then we'd return home like normal. I had no doubt, as sweat trickled down my sides and back, that I'd averted a crisis. Now, we just had to get home before dark.

I can't let him go, I thought to myself, that single idea burning into my brain. I glanced to the side and viewed New Haven once again, now to my right. I could even make out the baseball field where Nathaniel would play again soon. This time, I would cheer from the bleachers, no matter what migraine or illness I had to fight through. Such a great kid, hardworking, kind. *I can't lose him to that house.*

It had been years ago when I nearly lost myself to it. A much simpler time. Back when I still wore bright, colorful clothes, dozens of bracelets and necklaces, had a collection of bongs and pipes. Before Cliff and I were really adults, just a young couple in love. I explored New Haven with a sense of awe back then, having come from our big-city-college, following the man I'd fallen for. Back then, I always called him Ben, 'cause I preferred his real name over the nickname his friends gave him. Back then, I didn't have any scars on my legs and feet.

That house held many things in its depths. Horrible images, creeping threats, the worst nightmares that continued to haunt me. I'd been lucky to escape with my life, but I would never be the same, and I would never go back. Not for a million dollars. The house on the hill needed to stay abandoned, needed to be closed off for good. Whatever lived there, and still survived there, I couldn't bear the thought of it coming outside. Nobody in New Haven was prepared for something like that.

When I reached the top of the hill, I found Nathaniel sitting on the road, head in his hands. Next to him, his bike lay on the ground, useless. One of the tires had gone completely flat. He looked so disheartened, I felt another pang of regret for how rough I'd acted, and slowly walked over to him.

"I'm sorry, Nate." I frowned at the bike. "Got a flat?"

"I don't know how," he said, rubbing his forehead. "Just... popped as soon as I got up here." He closed his eyes and groaned. "We're so far from the house."

"Hey, it's okay. Come on." I offered him a hand, which he accepted. Once Nathaniel had climbed to his feet, I pulled out my phone. "I'll call Dad. Maybe he can..."

My voice trailed off. The screen said I had no service, and my fitness watch appeared to have lost GPS signal as well. "I don't have service."

While he studied his flat tire, I surveyed the hilltop. It looked much the same as earlier, still desolate of any other people and extremely quiet. Eerily quiet, in fact.

The forest was certainly darker now. I could barely see into the depths of the trees. The underbrush was too thick. As I searched the road for anything else, up and down both sides, I watched for the deer we'd seen earlier. I could use at least one friendly face.

"Totally flat," Nathaniel said, groaning. "Bet you wish I had a phone now, huh?"

"Oh my God..." I covered my mouth and pointed to what I'd seen. "Is that...?"

Up ahead, where the deer had stood, it now sprawled on the ground. The legs were sticking out at strange angles, blood had soaked into the grass around it. Those white spots on the doe's back were no longer pure. Guts were spread like toppings and flies collected around the neck area of the deer. The skin had been torn open, ripped apart. It was a mangled mess, impossible to tell where, exactly, the attack had concentrated. Or what had done it.

"Mom, maybe we should... get outta here." Nathaniel looked up at me, more afraid than ever. He stared so intently into my face I wondered if he was trying his hardest not to look at the deer anymore.

My own stomach churned. Less than ten minutes ago, that deer had been alive, peaceful. Whatever killed it — massacred it — was likely nearby. And I didn't want anything to do with that.

A flat tire, faulty service, and the carcass of a friendly doe. It was too much. It threatened to overwhelm me. I could so easily slip back into those frightful memories, the trauma I was always outrunning. But I peered into my son's face, steadied myself, and grasped hard for any solution. It was up to me now.

"Let's leave the bike," I said, trying to keep my voice steady, "and come back for it tomorrow." Those were the right words. I felt it immediately. But I went on, reaching for Nathaniel's head. "I'm really sorry I yelled at you. Let's just get back to the house, okay? Come on, trust me. We can make it."

"But how?" he whimpered.

Nathaniel took a few steps closer to me, stood pressed to my side. Night crept closer. It wasn't a calm darkness that fell on us. It was a cover for something worse, something lurking in those trees. All around us, the world shifted, and we were in the wild.

"Hop on my bike," I said. I balanced myself on the seat, as far forward as I could manage. "It'll be fine. Just uncomfortable. It'll have to work."

Nathaniel quickly clambered on behind me.

"Put your arms around me," I said. "You might have to run up the hills if we lose momentum."

He wrapped both arms around my midsection. I could feel

him shaking. I felt just as afraid, but it wasn't a time for fear. We needed to get moving. Casting one last look at the bike and then the corpse, I started to pedal. Slowly, at first. With enormous effort, leaning forward. We were halfway to the edge of the hill, the deer to our immediate left. If only we could start downhill, I'd feel a lot better.

Nathaniel screamed. "Mom, by the deer! Look!"

I whipped my head in that direction and saw it. Above the lifeless, bloody body, at the very edge of the trees, the underbrush was shaking violently. I thought I saw something glinting, like a knife or razor-sharp teeth. The shadows were too dark. I couldn't see what crouched there. But the bushes and leaves were rustling angrily. Nathaniel screamed again, right into my ears. Whatever it was, it started to emerge from the trees. A hulking beast, maybe. I turned away and pedaled harder, straight ahead, lunging for the descent.

"Hold on!" I yelled over the rushing wind.

Straight down, at breakneck speed, the bike flew down the road. All of our weight wobbled from side to side. I pleaded for it to be steady, to not crash. I couldn't look back, didn't dare. I just focused on balance, on speed. Nathaniel gripped me tighter as we whooshed down the hillside and yelled something about "moving faster!"

I tried not to think, just to act, to push ahead. The dark beast rushed beside us in the trees. The underbrush violent, like a tornado blew through it. I knew it was following. I could picture the glare of those teeth, sparkling in the rising moon, chasing along the roadside. Nathaniel mumbled incoherent prayers into my sweaty back. The wind picked up around us, swirling in the treetops, howling like a monster. There was no safety here. There wouldn't be for a long time, not until we reached home, but each hill would put us closer. Distance between us and that horrible house.

That house. I nearly lost control of the bike when I realized it. My eyes grew wide, my breathing turned shallow, and I understood.

Forcing my legs to another level of exertion, I managed to top the next hill with incredible speed. Every fiber of my lower body screamed in pain, but I thought about the scars on my ankles and the way that house had gripped at them. The way it sunk its teeth and its nails into my skin, pulling backward into the darkness. I would do anything to save Nathaniel from that fate. I would bike until my muscles exploded and veins burst.

"Do you see it?" I asked him. We were on top of the next hill now, but I didn't slow down.

Nathaniel shifted around, looking back. His voice trembled. "I... don't think so. Don't stop, Mom, please."

"I won't, honey." I gritted my teeth, taking deep, ragged breaths. "Not til we're home."

Without knowing if we'd truly escaped, I didn't stop until all the hills were behind us. The next few miles passed with chills and desperate glances into the trees, afraid we might see that beast once again, ready to pounce. A few times, I thought I saw a little glint of light in the woods on either side, but it never persisted.

We wound our way back along the road as night fell completely. There were no streetlights, only the glimmer of the moon. Nathaniel used my phone and held it out with the flashlight on, supposedly to "light the way," but I knew he was really afraid of this darkness.

Once we'd gone four or five miles and the landscape had become more recognizable, my mind started to wander. Both legs had gone numb for the most part, mindless oars that propelled the two of us toward safety. Nathaniel's face was buried in my back and had been for most of the trip. I used it as motivation, desperately pushing through fatigue and screeching pain to reach our home.

Part of me doubted whether safety really waited there. If we could find it anywhere in New Haven. A part of my mind, growing like a fungus, suspected the worst. It didn't make sense... the flat, phones not working, mutilated carcass. I replayed the list over and over in my mind, as well as the fire at George's shop. Coincidences? Or the sign I'd been watching for?

Ever since I'd escaped that terrible house, ever since I burst through the front door and into a strangled, blinding light, I had wondered and waited. Such a dark place would not—could not—sleep forever. It would eventually stir, I'd always known it. And when those doors opened, horrible things would emerge. Would hunt.

It wasn't time to freak out yet. But it was time to talk with Cliff. We needed to be on the same page, now more than ever, and we needed a plan in case things really turned bad. I thought about it the entire way home, up until we reached the gravel drive and Nathaniel stirred, rubbing his eyes.

"Did we make it?" he asked groggily, leaning his forehead against me.

"We're home."

I pulled into the grass and dismounted the bike. My legs gave out and I collapsed on the lawn, feeling dew against my face. I could've disappeared into that dirt, let it consume me. But Nathaniel knelt next to me. He put an arm around me, and I used him for support, struggling to my feet.

"Help me inside, will you? Thank you, baby."

As we neared the light of the kitchen and I hobbled across the porch, I couldn't help but peer in the direction of that abandoned house. The silhouette was small and dark, far away, but I no longer thought of it as dormant. One of the lights flashed on and then off, or maybe I imagined it. I didn't know anymore. I didn't know if it mattered.

That house, and its threat, had never been so awake. And it seemed to be moving closer.

CHAPTER 6
KAIA WOODS

Main Street wasn't very busy that day, but that's how I liked it. Allison and I were making our usual stops. It was our pattern, ever since high school, when we had an afternoon to kill and wanted to hang out in town, rather than at my house. — We rarely ever went to Allison's house when she lived with her mom, but that's just because she lived in town and they didn't have a backyard or a whole forest to explore like at my place.

Every storefront, restaurant, and anything else worth checking out was along Main Street. Most of the buildings — and the people inside them — had been there for decades, if not centuries. Every so often, we got some turnover. There was a plant shop that didn't last long, and it became an antique store. (We had three of those, more than any other type of store.) But beyond small changes like that, everything stayed basically the same.

So when Allison and I trekked along the sidewalk, following it for five blocks — between the police/fire station and the houses; the only interesting part of the road — it felt just like being in high school again. We made our way along one side, window shopping for the most part. Yes, I wanted to get out of New

Haven, but I still appreciated it. Never had to worry about things changing in New Haven. I would always have this Allison and idyllic Main Street.

There was one store that sold mostly clothes, with a toy area in the back for kids, and I liked it because they usually had some vintage stuff. I didn't find anything there, but Allison picked out a sweater she adored.

"It's literally ninety-five degrees outside," I laughed as she held it up, inspecting it.

"*I know,* but I can save it for fall." Allison held it against herself and cocked her head. "What do you think?"

It was a vintage sweater with alternating patterns in rows, almost like a Christmas sweater, but with a burnt orange color and a gray stretch across the middle. It wasn't something I particularly liked, but Allison had a way of making anything look good. Unfair, really.

"Looks good on you," I said truthfully.

"Eh, I dunno."

She waffled over the sweater for a while longer and decided not to buy it. We left the store and continued down the road, passing the biggest antique shop in town, with two stories of old junk nobody wanted anymore. Anytime we browsed in there, it was all old people, besides me and Allison. (And the noisy kids who only came in to play the skeeball game in the back.) But neither of us felt like it today.

We weren't *really* looking to buy anything. Just like in high school—only then it was because we didn't have money—the two of us enjoyed strolling up and down this street for the atmosphere, for each other. I loved being in New Haven with Allison, commenting on funny display items, or the older couple who always drove around their antique car, one of those really slick ones from the 70s.

A little ways past the big antique store, we passed the side-road that led to the baseball field. The block right before it had a boutique store and the one right after a sports bar and grill. Neither of these were any interest to us, so we strolled by them, barely glancing over.

New Haven seemed like the kind of place where there was nothing, and that was true if you weren't paying attention. But one time, when it was getting dark, we saw a deer walking right up Main Street. That's the kind of thing you don't get anywhere else.

Or the beige-colored, abandoned brick building on one end of town — some sort of forgotten factory, I think — where people would draw the wackiest graffiti. I saw this one, a huge monkey smoking a banana, 'til they removed it a couple days later. I guess other places have graffiti, but that still makes me laugh.

All that stuff we would've missed if not for our walks together. Sometimes just being present is enough. That's why we loved to spend our wasted hours strolling up and down New Haven.

We came to the last block before the street turned into small houses, an old playground, and the abandoned building. The sidewalk along here was cracked and shoots of grass peeked out. George's shop — where it had been — was straight ahead of us, a charred area, dirt-black, sticking out like a sore thumb from the rest of the street. There was another antique store on that same block. The owner had been friends with George. I didn't want to think about any of that.

"Wanna cross here?" I suggested.

Allison looked ahead, where some of the residue still littered the grass-speckled sidewalk and the building's sides were caked in something dark. It wasn't hard to imagine the flames, ripping through that family and throwing the whole town into chaos.

"Yeah. We should."

The two of us crossed the road — "Not many cars out today," Allison said — and headed back the way we'd come. This side didn't have as many stores; there was an old-fashioned diner ahead, some insurance office, and a pizza/wings restaurant beyond that, which was probably going out of business soon. Most of the storefronts on this side were vacant, torn-up rooms behind empty display cases.

Up ahead, I recognized the oldest Dawes kid stumbling out of the diner. He had three of those white, grease-soaked bags in his hands and bulky headphones over his ears. I couldn't remember his name, but he trudged in our direction, head down. As we got closer, I heard him humming to himself, a low sound, but sweet.

My mom had told me about him. Smith, I think, was his name. She said the church ladies prayed for him all the time because he was the sweetest kid but out of place in this town. Mom called him "a fish out of water." With his eyes glued to the ground and those huge headphones, I felt sorry for him. He seemed timid, even afraid, of everything around him.

We were about to pass him, in front of an alleyway, when a big, shiny truck pulled out. Smith nearly stepped in its path, but the truck blared its horn, and the boy almost fell over backward. He dropped all three of his greasy bags, just as someone from inside the truck roared at him, laughing. Smith hung his head and stood in place, taking the abuse silently. Then the truck pulled out onto Main Street, spewing that disgusting diesel exhaust.

I rushed across the alleyway, leaving Allison for a moment,

and started grabbing a few of his tightly-wrapped burgers, which had rolled into the street.

"Hey, those are mine," he huffed.

I held them out toward him, offering my kindest possible smile. "Here. I didn't want you to lose 'em."

"Oh." He shuffled in place, avoiding my eyes. Finally, he extended one of the bags, still not making eye contact.

I dropped the burgers inside. "Dinner for your family?"

He nodded, stiffly, staring at the ground.

"My brother's on your baseball team," I said, my arms hanging at my sides. "Nate."

His eyes flicked over my face for just a minute, then back to the sidewalk. There were a few stray fries sitting there. "Yes. He... I like him."

"Well, enjoy your dinner," I said, not sure how exactly to close this conversation. I stepped back, and Allison moved to my side. Again, I offered my warmest smile.

Smith jerked his head, watching from the corner of his eyes. "Thank you."

He shuffled away, toward the east side of town and didn't look back. When he'd gotten a few steps away from us, he started humming again, hiding his face. I don't think he ever met my eyes.

"Isn't that the new, weird kid?" Allison asked.

I frowned at her. "You shouldn't call him weird."

"Sorry, I just meant—"

"I know." We started walking again, passing by the diner and the insurance office, with plenty of vacant storefronts thrown in. "People call someone 'weird' so they don't have to feel bad about being awful to them. Don't you think it should be the opposite? The 'weird' people are the ones we should be the kindest to. And everyone who actually knows Smith says he's really nice."

"Yeah, you're right." Allison chewed her lip. "He's new to town. I think that's why people call him weird."

"So what? I don't think where you're born has any impact on what kind of person you are."

"He did seem nice."

"Of course he did. He's just a person. Not a... weirdo. People here" —I gestured vaguely around Main Street— "act like they know everything, but I bet there's a lot we could learn from someone like Smith."

After that, we moved in silence for a minute. I could've gotten angry with Allison, but I think she didn't know any better. She'd only seen things from a New Haven perspective. She didn't have a mom who could tell her about the world outside of this strange community. And it's not like Allison was a hateful person. She never had been. If she was, I wouldn't have been such good friends with her.

I figured, after our interaction with Smith, she would never call him weird or anything like that again.

It had been a day pretty similar to this, hot and dry, the summer before our eighth grade year. Allison and I hadn't been friends for super long, and it'd been one of our first times hanging out in public together. We'd gone to the pizza place with some friends and then split off to go shopping at the antique store.

Well, there were a lot of people around, crowding up the sidewalks. And this older man—I'd never seen him before—felt the need to come talk to us. He was being pretty creepy, and as a thirteen-year-old the whole thing caught me off guard. He tried to grab my shoulder at one point, and I slapped his hand away.

The guy went crazy on me. Started spewing all sorts of terrible, racist, misogynistic bullshit. I hadn't even *heard* half the things he said, because nobody had really acted racist toward me in New Haven before. (My mom's got some stories, though.) I was stunned, honestly, and trying not to cry.

Well, Allison freaking punched the old guy right in his face. He stumbled back, and she shouted at him, "Leave my friend alone, you pig, you're fucking trash," that kind of stuff. I just stared in awe. It was so unexpected, the kind of thing you'd see in a movie. Allison, out of nowhere, became my favorite person.

I knew better afterward. My mom had a talk with me, and I knew if somebody tried it again I'd stand up for myself. But at the time, I was so confused and scared, it meant the world to me. Allison didn't ever get angry, and knowing she would pop off like that, for me, just gave me a sense of security around her. I could trust her. I loved her.

As we strolled through New Haven, Allison caught me grinning to myself.

"What is it?" she asked.

"Oh, nothing." I beamed at her. "Just thinking how lucky I am to have you."

"Pshh, whatever." Allison rolled her eyes, showing her pearly whites. "You're just lucky to have me for fashion advice."

"Okay, *no*," I laughed. "I definitely have better style than you."

"No way. You wear overalls sometimes."

"Overalls are cute!"

"Yeah, *okay*, farm girl."

I socked her in the shoulder, both of us chuckling, and continued on our way.

Ever since that day, she'd been my closest friend, by far. And after high school, my only real one. Everyone else did their own thing, and when you don't see people at school every day and they aren't forced to be in the same place as you, they don't have any desire to stay in touch. I guess it's sad, but I was the same way. I didn't need them. Only Allison.

"I'm gonna head home once we get to the car," Allison said, checking the time on her phone. "Gotta make dinner."

"Gotcha." I felt a little deflated. This was the first time I'd seen Allison since her wedding, because anytime I asked to hang out she'd been busy. And we'd only been here for about an hour. Was I doomed to see her for an hour a week or less the rest of our lives?

Malaki. He doesn't even appreciate her.

Maybe things in New Haven could change. They seemed to be changing for the worse.

"Are you alright, Kaia?"

I shook away those thoughts and forced a smile. "Yeah." I pointed to the next block ahead of us. "Can we stop in that crystal store?"

"Sure." Allison rolled her eyes. "You and your crystals, huh?"

The crystal store had popped up around four years ago, boasting an assortment of crystals, various rocks, incense, tie-dye shirts and flags, and more. Besides Allison, the "hippie store" was the main reason I didn't hate growing up in New Haven. The old lady who owned it was always very kind; it helped that she was friends with Mom and gave me discounts on everything.

"Girl, you know it's the best store in New Haven."

"Not much competition."

"Okay, but still."

She raised her eyebrows. "Even counting the big antique story with the skeeball machines?"

"Yeah, I like the hippie store better."

"Because you're a wannabe hippie."

"Whatever." I tossed my hair dramatically. "I get good discounts."

"How many crystals do you have now? Like a hundred?"

"*No,* not a hundred." I laughed and punched her lightly in the shoulder.

Allison smirked. "Hey, I mean, it's cute, just a little obsessive."

"Girl, shut up. You're the jealous one."

A few minutes later, we entered the store. A long counter stretched out on the left-hand side. On the right, there was a wall of crystals (tiny fluorite, huge azurite, some individually labeled, others in a box with a hundred of the same kind, quartz necklaces, some you could make a necklace with) that I headed straight for. In the back of the store, they had clothing, decorations, and this is what Allison shuffled toward, making tiny movements. She always got oddly rigid when we came in here, like she didn't think she belonged. But I didn't worry about that; I was focused on the countless crystals in front of me.

Maybe I should buy one for her, I mused. I could buy her one that correlated to her birthday, but that seemed kind of basic. And she wouldn't care if I bought one and said, "it's supposed to help with stress," or anything like that. If only they had a crystal that would help you deal with your new, asshole husband…

"Hello, Kaia."

I spun around and found the old lady behind the counter, nodding at me. She wore a loose, flowing shirt and wrinkles, as well as a bright, friendly smile.

"Hi, Ms. Hargrave. How's it going?" I asked.

"All is well." She sighed. "You're my first customer today."

"Oh..." I felt bad and picked up an amethyst to inspect. "Well, seems like a slow day for everyone."

"Let me know if you need help, yes? And tell Naomi I said hello."

"Will do." I tried to offer my most sympathetic nod. "Thank you."

I returned to browsing, vaguely aware of Allison, in the corner of my eye. She stood in the back of the store, ruffling through some of the hoodies.

"You are Kaia's friend?"

"Yeah. I'm Allison."

"Yes, I think I recognize you."

I glanced over to find Ms. Hargrave standing behind her counter still, peering intently at Allison.

"You seem to... have a negative force around you." She frowned. This wasn't her usual, business persona, and she spoke in a low tone. "Darling, are you feeling okay?"

"Yeah, I'm fine." Allison furrowed her eyebrows and glanced at me, confusion etched in her forehead. "Just... looking at these drug rugs."

"The Baja hoodies are our most popular." Ms. Hargrave shook her head. "No, I... would you be interested in a tarot card reading? For free, of course."

"No, I'm really not." Allison smiled weakly and started moving toward me. "Sorry."

"It's in your best interest," she pressed on. "There is something... something around you. A negative energy."

"Yeah, you said. But I'm alright," Allison stepped toward me briskly. She lowered her head and whispered, "I'm gonna wait outside." Then she left the store.

I collected the amethyst crystal I'd decided on and also a clear quartz. With these in hand, I moved to the register, where Ms. Hargrave was waiting.

"I didn't mean to offend her," she began, sadly.

I handed her the crystals and shrugged. "It's okay. She's not really into... all this." I gestured around the store. "Can I get one of those necklace strings, too?"

"Yes, of course, dear." She cleared her throat and packaged the crystals for me, wrapping them carefully. "But your friend, Kaia... I meant what I said. There's a negative energy around her. Perhaps following her. I... I felt it right when she looked at me."

"I'll keep an eye on her, Ms. Hargrave." I offered her a twenty-dollar bill and smiled.

She pushed the two, small packages toward me and nodded, muttering something to herself.

"Keep the change," I said, grabbing my purchases. "Thanks, Ms. Hargrave. See you around."

"Goodbye, Kaia."

I emerged onto the sidewalk and found Allison shifting from side to side, staring into the empty storefront which sat beside the crystal store. It had been empty for as long as I could remember, but Dad swore there used to be a small arcade there. I didn't believe him.

—The humidity swamped me right away, and I couldn't wait to get back to her air-conditioned car.

"You okay?" I asked.

We started down the sidewalk toward her car, parked a few blocks down. Allison nodded. "Yeah. That old lady was really after me."

"She's a lot, but she's sweet." I opened one of my packages and found the clear quartz, as well as the necklace string. "If I gave you a necklace, would you wear it?"

Allison hesitated. "What, you're worried about 'bad energy' or whatever, too?"

"No, I just wanna give you a gift." I frowned and pocketed everything I'd bought. "Nevermind."

"I'm sorry, Kaia. I would, yes." Allison kicked at the sidewalk. "I'm just in a mood."

"Are you doing okay? With… Malaki and everything?"

She sighed and didn't answer right away. Allison fished out her key fob and clicked it twice. Up ahead, her car chirped in its spot.

"I'm okay, yeah. Don't worry about it."

"Fine, I won't worry, *if* you accept my gift. I'll give it to you next time I see you."

"Okay, deal." Allison rubbed her forehead, groaning. "I think I should've bought one of those hippie hoodies. There was this one I really liked. Wanna buy me that, too?"

"Hell no." I laughed and waited as she went around to the driver's side door. "Who's the wannabe hippie now?"

CHAPTER 7
NAOMI WOODS

We didn't return for the bike until the next afternoon, by which point the hills were baking in the sun and the green grass had turned a dirtier, dried-out color. New Haven needed some rain. And some answers.

Nathaniel climbed into the passenger seat of my car, a green Chevy Malibu, and I could tell he was already afraid. Though he walked with his chest out, his chin drooped and that youthful face gave away every thought inside. Or maybe as his mom I could read him easily. Either way, I felt certain he didn't want to go, but he put on a brave face anyway.

So did I. We couldn't hide from this fear forever.

"Thanks for letting me sleep a while," I said as he bucked his seatbelt. I stifled a yawn and leaned back against the headrest for a moment as cool air from the vents bathed me. "It was a long night."

"I couldn't fall asleep," he admitted, fumbling with the seam of his jeans. He didn't meet my gaze, so I started rolling down the driveway.

"Me either." I reached out and tousled his hair. "It's gonna be okay, Nate."

No answer.

As the car progressed, it kicked up dust behind us. After a few days of intense heat and no precipitation, New Haven became more and more like a parched throat. Gravel would let loose all of its dust and the fields would dry up and blow aimlessly in the wind. Clouds would come and go but never quench the earth's thirst. I'd mostly gotten used to the summers here, the sudden switch between a week of storms and a week of drought, but sometimes it caught me off guard. Even after two decades here.

It was only a ten-minute drive to the place where we'd left the bike, but it felt like so much longer. Retracing my path from the night before brought with it horrible flashbacks and the type of throat-clenching anxiety I hadn't felt in years. Sleep deprivation certainly didn't help, but I had no choice. Staying up past sunrise and catching a few hours of rest in the late morning had been the only option. The only way to feel safe last night.

When we'd returned home from the panic-inducing escape, Cliff had been fast asleep, not that it surprised me. That explained why he hadn't called or anything. I didn't want to wake him, but I also couldn't climb into bed peacefully, not after… everything. So instead, I brewed a pot of coffee, turned on the television just for some company, and waited on the couch all night. Waiting for something to scratch at the door or a face to appear in the window. I sat, back straight as a log, until sunlight snuck through the window and touched my cheeks. With the doors and windows all locked, and a kitchen knife on the table beside me, I maintained that position for hours. Then Cliff finally stumbled into the conjoined kitchen/living room area and spotted me.

He rubbed his eyes groggily, picking at the gunk, and reached for my shoulder. "Are you okay, honey? Why are you up?"

Right away, I shook my head and started to sob.

But the beginning of the day is never a great time for a breakdown, so I couldn't explain myself fully in that moment. We planned on having the conversation later, hopefully that night, but for now those emotions were bottled up, straining against my skull. It gave me a splitting headache, only numbed slightly by Ibuprofen, Tylenol, and coffee.

Cliff hadn't yet told me everything Jeremy had said, so I expected some mutual info sharing whenever that time came. Until then, Nathaniel and I would retrieve the bike and take another look at the area where we'd seen that shadowy figure and his beautiful victim.

I slowed the car as we approached the top of the hill where everything had started to unravel. Instinctually, I glanced to the right, but there was no deer carcass. In fact, there were no signs of it at all. No blood in the grass, no stray pieces of flesh, no flies. I almost couldn't believe my eyes until Nathaniel spoke up.

"So, that's all... gone?" He craned his neck for a better view and then turned to me with disbelief. "Kinda weird..." He laughed nervously.

"Do you see the bike?" I asked him, inching down the road.

He pointed up ahead. "Mom, look."

I followed his gesture through the front windshield and saw it right where we'd left it. Only now both tires were ripped to shreds, the frame itself had been bent in half, curled up almost. I couldn't imagine the strength it would take to bend a metal bike like that. Now that I looked intently, it had actually moved a little closer to the tree line. The handlebars were sticking into some vegetation.

"That's... not good." I looked at Nathaniel, who was

chewing on his nails.

"Can we just leave it?" he asked, eyes pleading with me. "I don't... I don't wanna get that close to the trees."

I smiled at him and started to turn around. "You're right. It looks trashed anyway. Let's just head back. Maybe we can buy you a new bike this weekend."

<> <> <>

What little courage I built during the daylight hours was dashed to pieces when the sun fell. That house on the far away hill always flexed its power over me at night. It would send a flashback of horror or a migraine or a shiver, and there I would be again. Only now, I wasn't alone. It wanted me and my son.

My friend, Susan, she and I called once a week or chatted at church (though I hadn't been going). She told me to try to relax that day, talk things over with Cliff. So I did just that and finally had a conversation with him. But I knew she probably thought I'd imagined the hulking figure. And damn it, maybe I had, but that didn't mean there wasn't a very real threat. Waiting inside that goddamn house.

"Nate said he wanted to get closer to it," I explained, looking from the carpet floor to my husband. I was seated on the couch, one elbow propped on the armrest, supporting my head with a feeble hand. "I yelled at him so he wouldn't go. He went back up the hill, toward home, and that's when everything happened."

Cliff sat on the opposite edge of the couch, his eyes glazed over, certainly picturing everything I'd described. The television in front of us cast strange shadows around the room, deepening the age lines on his face. I watched as he didn't move. His hands were in a triangle shape, pressed up against his mouth, brain churning.

While we sat in the dark living room, only the television offering light, I told him all about the bike ride from the evening before. The deer carcass, losing phone service, Nathaniel's flat tire. I even mentioned seeing something in the forest, though now I was less certain it had been a beast—that might've been my terrified imagination. And in a roundabout way, I ended with the most throat-clenching part of the whole ordeal. The part that scared me just as much now as it had then. As soon as I saw Nathaniel staring up at the house, in its shadow and grip, I couldn't stop thinking about it.

"He can't go…" I leaned forward and gripped my knees, knuckles turning pale, trying to keep my voice low. Nathaniel was in bed, supposedly asleep, and Kaia in her room. Both of them roomed upstairs, but I didn't want to chance them overhearing. Not right now. "It would… it would kill me to lose him. That house, Ben. He wouldn't have a…"

He turned to face me, offering a hand. I wanted to reach out and take hold of it, but my arms wouldn't budge. I didn't feel brave enough to let go of my knees, to emerge from the ball I'd formed. It took all my restraint to stay still, to not panic. This was how it'd felt years ago, too. This was trauma unburying itself and emerging from the grave.

Cliff moved closer to me, placing an arm around my shoulder. I fell into him, pushed my body against his, wanted so badly to blend together. I didn't want to carry this burden alone anymore. It had been years of weighing on me, and it would be years more, alone. I could only lean against him, rigid and stiff. He massaged my back and shoulders with his gentle, strong hands. I tried to breathe deeply, I tried not to break down again.

There was no sound except for the faint television, though neither of us paid any attention. No noises drifted from the outside. Our farm had gone quiet, the air asleep. Sometimes the house itself would groan, and I'd shudder at the thought of a stranger on the staircase. —I tried not to think about that anymore.

"You made the right choice to get out of there," Cliff said at last, breaking the prolonged silence. He continued massaging my back, offering his touch and maximum support. "Nate's a smart kid. He knows better, especially now. I'm sure he's scared, too."

I nodded, trying to sink into comfort. I wasn't on the verge of crying, but the tears would sometimes slip through. Long ago, I'd stopped sobbing. I was more likely to scream or have another panic attack. The only way to deal with something was to stare it in the face, but then it would overwhelm me. As a little girl and a teenager, I'd seen awful things, racist things. And then everything with that house... Crying had never helped before, and it certainly wouldn't now. So instead I fought myself.

"What happened with the fire in town?" I asked, my voice cold and determined. It was time to start digging, time to start planning. "Did you find out?"

"Are you sure you wanna talk about that right now?" Cliff asked. He gave up on the massage and instead held me close against his chest. I liked that better.

"Yeah." I gulped. "Just tell me. I think I can guess."

"Well... the fire was pretty big. You could see the smoke all over town. Lots of people rushed over to help, of course, and they brought out all three fire trucks. Just to stop it from spreading, really. There was no hope for the shop, Jeremy said." Cliff peered straight ahead now, into the dark corner of the room, as if replaying the entire episode in his mind. I watched him carefully, his jaw as it moved, his eyes.

"And George?"

Cliff shook his head. "Found his body inside. His boy right beside him."

I pressed my face into his chest and shivered. "That's terrible, Ben."

He chewed on his next words for a second and nodded slowly. I could feel his heartbeat against my cheek, and it quickened. "Yeah, it is. Even worse... Jeremy says they don't think it was an accident. Not sure how the fire started yet, but the two bodies... they didn't look right or something. I dunno what the sheriff told him or how they figured it out, but Jeremy claims they were tied up."

"Ben, look at me." I turned my head upward and reached for his neck, drawing his face closer to mine. "You talked with the sheriff, right?"

He met my eyes now, inquisitive. "He was there, yeah."

I nodded. "And did he mention that new family in town? The Dawes?"

Cliff looked taken aback. He cocked his head, silent for a moment. "Yeah, he did, but... how'd you know that?"

I sat up now, still close to him, and frowned. I'd been afraid of this. "That family, the Dawes... they're the nicest people, honey. Anne — the mom — she's been at the women's meetings at church recently. Widow, looking for a fresh start. And I *knew* he'd instantly connect them to the fire, because he did that kinda thing to me when we moved here."

Cliff's eyes were even wider now. He started pulling at his chin hairs, the way he always did. "What are you talking about?"

"He was awful to me when we first moved here, anytime you weren't around. Sheriff Wheeler, he doesn't trust anyone who comes here. Especially not when you look like me, but even if you look like Anne." I shook my head and tried to stop myself from yelling. "It's... anybody new, anybody out-of-town. He could... Well, Susan's the only one who stood up for me. I'm gonna make sure Anne has more people to stand up for her."

Cliff opened his mouth to speak, but I shushed him with a finger.

I reached for his hand and held it in mine, tight. "He's gonna go after them, but I swear they're the nicest people. You gotta believe me. Their boy, Smith, he's on the baseball team with Nate. Just keep an eye on the sheriff. I don't want him to try anything, okay? Just keep an eye on him, you and Jeremy. For anything... shady."

"I will, baby." He leaned closer to kiss my forehead.

I stood from the couch, pulling his hand. "Let's go outside for a minute. I wanna ask you something." With the TV at my back, I must have looked like a spooky silhouette, but I kept pulling until he rose to his feet. I glanced around the room, peered into the black depths of the hallway, and then gestured at the front door.

Once he was standing, I led him. The floor creaked under our weight and the television played mindless commercials. We had important things to discuss, but it needed to be out there, on the porch. When no children emerged from the house's depths, I opened the front door and stepped out into the night.

The single light on our front porch was out, and I left it. Might actually help. Instead, I walked straight to the railing, letting go of his hand. Leaning against the wood, I could stare out at the shadowy field and the sky. It was a deep shade of purple but off in the distance, above the oak forest, it turned slightly lighter where the sun had been. There was a bold, bright moon casting a spotlight on our driveway, and stars twinkling in the distance.

"It's kinda cold out here," Cliff remarked, moving next to me.

I pulled both his arms around me and stood with my back pressed against his front. The two of us stayed like that for a minute, feeling a cool breeze against our cheeks as it lifted my hair into his face. The big oak tree in our backyard rustled. It was a peaceful night, as it often was this far from town. But I worried that might change soon.

"Should we talk to the kids about all of this?" I asked him at last, not looking back. My voice was low as we stared into the forever distance and wondered what needed to be done. "Tell them to avoid that house, stay in touch with us, all of that? I just… I want us to have a plan."

"Do you think they'll even try to go up there?" Cliff asked, placing both hands on my stomach and drawing me closer.

"Nate almost did. And I don't wanna risk it." I leaned back and breathed in his aftershave. I no longer felt I was teetering on the edge of panic. Just concerned and uncertain. "And I just… don't want them to be caught off guard if something happens."

Cliff buried his lips in my hair, taking deep, meaningful breaths. An unspoken sentence passed before he answered. "We can have that talk with them, you're right, we should. But…" A deep breath. "Not yet. Let's give it a week. Maybe things will die down after this. Maybe it'll pass."

I sighed and rubbed the back of his hands, still on my midsection. It was what I'd expected him to say, and I already had a response packaged. "Alright, hun, that's fine. There's something else I need to tell you, though… The real reason I wanted to talk out here."

I moved in his arms and turned to face him. We stared into each other's eyes, barely visible in the darkness. His were curious, thinking. Behind him, the table and chairs on our porch were silhouettes, barely existing.

This was the part where I hoped to change his mind. Cliff didn't understand the threat, not quite. But that would change right now.

"Follow me," I said. Then I led him around to the side of the wrap-around porch.

Our footsteps were small and noisy, breaking the still air. As we moved, I peered into the distance, trying to make out the distorted silhouette on the far line of hills. It was barely visible from here, especially at night, but I had a feeling it would do fine. You didn't need to see much of the house to understand.

"Look at the house," I said, pointing to it, "and listen to me."

Cliff did as he was told, leaning over the railing a few inches, eyeing that beast with disdain, mistrust. But not fear, not yet. As he waited for me to continue, I took a few steps back, for dramatic purposes, and watched his expression.

"At that church meeting, the women in town, they told me some things. A few of them are real night owls, and they say they often look out. At that house." I cleared my throat and went on. "According to them, Ben, if you watch it at night, you'll feel it. You'll see it." I turned to look at it myself, moved next to him, so that we were standing side-by-side, observing the ghostly shape.

"They've seen movement in the house. Flickering lights, with shadows in front of them. They live much closer than us, of course, and so they can *hear* things, too. And they've heard something up there, okay? Something inhuman. Almost like a scream. It was worrying me. I didn't want to believe it. I don't want to relive that night, to go through the nightmares again, but I needed to know, Ben. So, I came out here last night, when I couldn't sleep, and I watched it for a while. And... well, Ben..."

He swallowed so hard I could hear it. His hand crawled to

mine and it was shaking. Cliff looked at me, eyes wide. "What did you see, Naomi?"

I didn't answer. Instead, I placed a finger over his lips and then pointed it at the house again. His eyes followed like a magnet, across the farmlands and the treetops, up the distant hillside and that steep ascent. All the way to the pitch-black, house on the hill.

Only it wasn't so dark anymore. On the third floor of that decaying building, a light flickered behind one of the windows. It was feeble, barely there, but in the night it stood out like a horrible beacon. Even from so far away. The two of us stared and couldn't turn from it. It could have been a man or a woman or a child, of any size or shape. But one thing was for certain. It stood by the window, and it faced outward. Something. Something was there. And it stared down at New Haven from the bowels of that godforsaken building.

"I had another nightmare," I admitted to him, one arm wrapped around his. Cliff didn't answer, and I wasn't expecting him to. He seemed too stunned to speak, so I went on in a whisper. "And you know what? I figured something out."

He replied feebly, "Y- yeah?"

"I think I know what the house wants. What that thing's looking for." I shook my head at the thought and closed my eyes, but even there the figure watched me. It grew larger. "I think it's looking for another victim."

CHAPTER 8
IN NEW HAVEN

The sleek convertible whipped around bends in the country road, kicking up more dust with each speed increase. Another vehicle, a truck, roared around the corner, but Malaki simply swerved to the side at the last moment, running his tires into the grass and sending his car into a lurch. Then he ripped the steering wheel back to the left and continued to glide down the road, going even faster, daring anything to get in the way.

"Hell, yeah!" Malaki threw his head back with laughter, long hair falling over his shoulders. He wore sleek sunglasses and held onto the steering wheel with just one hand, the other dangling outside the car.

The passenger seat was empty, though that wasn't how he'd prefer it. Allison was at home, preparing dinner, which *was* how he wanted it. But as for his empty seat, if he could've filled it with anybody in town, he'd choose Kaia in an instant. The real reason he made his way into town now was the chance of seeing her, just a glimpse. Daring drives on the backroads were plenty fun, but every encounter with Kaia made his heart race like nothing else.

Not that she'd ever shown any interest in him. Hell, she'd refused him two or three times, anytime he made a serious move, which happened every couple of years. But that didn't matter, not to him. He was never *not* thinking of her, always pictured her in his mind, desperately wanted to feel her smooth, darker skin and wake up to that head full of curls on his pillow. Something about her smile, the way she carried herself, allured him. Kaia was irresistible, bold, fierce. Exactly what he wanted.

Malaki's convertible picked up speed until it neared the center of town. He passed the blackened heap of ashes and bricks where George's shop had been only a week earlier. Dust had collected on its surface now, as it did everything out here, blowing from all directions at all times. Without giving the tragedy a second thought, he moved past the site and started looking for parking spaces.

"Oh, damn!" He perked up, noticing a smooth-walking, magnetic girl just a few blocks down. He'd recognize Kaia from any angle.

Acting on instinct, he whipped his convertible into a parking space on the side of the road and climbed out, not bothering to open the door. Then he dropped to a crouch beside it, using his side mirror as he combed back his hair and gave himself a confident, sly grin. At last, straightening, he made his way to the sidewalk and started speed-walking in her direction.

"Hey, Kaia!" he called. She didn't turn around, so he broke into a short jog and finally came near enough to reach out and touch her arm. "Kaia, hey, it's me."

She shifted away and turned around, eyes narrowed. But she smiled a little bit at least. "What do you want, Malaki?"

"Oh, you know, just in town." He fell into stride beside her and noticed she was carrying a plastic bag, probably from a small shopping trip. "Oh, want me to carry that?"

He reached for the bag, but she switched it to her opposite

hand, further from him. "No, I'm fine."

She moved a few inches away from him, closer to the edge of the sidewalk. Malaki had an awful image of her tripping on a rock, stumbling into the road, and a car flattening her right before his eyes. But he also pictured himself saving her from that disaster, instantly becoming a hero—her hero. At the thought, and what might happen after, he couldn't help but grin.

"What are you smiling at?" she asked, raising an eyebrow.

"Nothing, nothing. What're you up to today?" Malaki reached out and tried to touch her back, but she squirmed away when he did so. *Maybe she likes it?* "You wanna come over later? Allison's making... something good, I assume."

Kaia gritted her teeth and held up the bag. He noticed now that it contained groceries. "Can't. Have to make dinner myself."

"Oh, well then maybe I'll come—"

"No, Malaki." They reached the edge of the block and paused for a moment as three cars rushed past. Kaia glanced across the street and started to move away from him. "I've gotta go, Nate's at baseball practice. I'm getting him and heading home. So I'll... see ya around."

Malaki stood, stunned, as she gave him a simple, half-hearted wave and then crossed the road. He waited at that intersection for a solid five minutes, as passersby avoided him and others stopped to share his company for just a moment. It was like time moved infinitely slow as Kaia strolled away, her beautiful body disappearing into a side street. When she was no longer in view, he felt his lust devolve into instant, visceral bitterness.

"God damn it." He looked down at his hands and saw they were clasped tight. Hair fell into his eyes, and his sunglasses were askew. He fixed his appearance, moving across the street finally, and changed his mind about evening plans.

I'm not going home for that bitch's cooking, he thought to himself, shuffling over the crosswalk. *I'll go get drunk.*

With his mind decided and his shoulders slouched, Malaki followed his own footsteps to the bar nearby where he knew they wouldn't ID him. The owner didn't have a problem with underage drinking, as long as he knew you and liked you. For Malaki, it was heaven, and for the barkeep it was another steady customer. At least *someone* appreciated his presence, even if he had to pay for that kind of attention.

Malaki entered the bar, leaving behind the putrid heat for a damp and dank stool, and did a quick once-over of the place. It was just as dusty and dingy as he'd remembered, the booths filled with unsavory, hairy men, and the barstools a mixture of folks. He noticed at the very end an extremely pretty blonde girl was seated all alone, two empty spots from anybody else. Malaki thought about heading over, but he expected she, too, was undeserving of him. So instead, he pocketed his sunglasses, yanked out his wallet, and headed to the opposite end.

There are only two good seats in a bar, he thought, claiming an empty stool for himself. *The ones next to the pretty girls and the ones where they can't see you watching.*

Chuckling to himself, Malaki tapped on the counter impatiently and waited for somebody to tend to him.

"Hey there!" Dusty sidled over, embracing Malaki's hand with his larger, meatier, sweaty one. "Long time no see, eh, pal? What're you drinking?"

"Something hard, Dusty." Malaki groaned and placed a hand to his forehead dramatically. "I'm all outta luck."

"Eh, I've got some lucky liquor here, don't ya worry." Dusty tapped his own forehead, as if he held all the secrets, and moved away to grab a large glass that would soon be filled.

Malaki took this chance to peer down the bar and observe the blonde girl, trying to guess at her drink. She looked sad, in a good way, and she would've been perfect for him. He knew it already. They could've been soulmates and had beautiful children and raucous sex late into the night. If only it wasn't for his goddamn wife and the home-cooked meal waiting for him. Well, by the time he ate it, he'd be absolutely hammered, if not black-out drunk. That would show her and all of them. That would prove his point. —And it made for a nice excuse.

"What's a'matter, huh?" Dusty plopped the drink on the counter, some of it sloshing over the sides. "This'll fix you up, no doubt."

"You ever had problems with women?" Malaki gulped down a fourth of the glass and shuddered as it hit him. He wiped his mouth and eyed the bartender. "Kind that won't appreciate ya?"

"Oh, sure, loads of 'em." Dusty wiped his hands on a towel that hung from his waist and stretched his back. "You know what I say? Their loss, man. Just forget about 'em." He winked at Malaki and moved further down the bar.

Malaki watched as Dusty approached the blonde girl and handed her a bill. She didn't glance down the bar in his direction even a single time, but Malaki didn't take his eyes off her. As she collected her belongings and rose from the barstool, he stared at her long legs, itching to call out or make a move. When he reexamined her face, he noticed her staring back at him, with a mixture of disgust and confusion. Malaki quickly put his head down and focused on the murky contents of his glass.

He heard the bell on the door jingle as she exited. Her presence evaporated and the rushing sounds of the bar overtook him. Murmurs from the booths and the clink of glasses on tables, on each other. Laughter and hushed tones, life and death. Malaki didn't raise his head, not even when Dusty had given him two more glasses and both were emptied. Time passed in a blur as he waited for anything to happen, drinking himself into a deeper state of self-pity.

The barstool beside him scratched against the floor and he heard the groan of a different man clambering onto it. At first, Malaki didn't look over, because he didn't really care about strangers, not even those sitting next to him, unless they were pretty. And from the sound and smell of him, this was a very un-pretty man.

When it came, the voice was cold, gravelly, and worn thin. "I've seen you around town, I think."

Malaki turned his head slightly. The man was old and wrinkled, shirt hanging from his boney shoulders, a ragged beard around his chin. His untamed eyebrows rose and he picked at something in his teeth, studying Malaki.

"So what?" Malaki huffed, reaching for his glass again. He realized it was empty and set it back down.

The old man grinned and gestured at it. "I'll buy you a few more if you agree to talk with me."

Malaki wrinkled his nose and mulled over his options. "Why? What d'you want with me?"

"I think you can help me with somethin', see," the old man said, offering a quick wink. "Let's leave it at that for now."

When Dusty swept by again, the old man ordered himself a drink and refilled Malaki's. Dusty gave the pair of them a skeptical, knowing look but kept to himself and moved past. The old man took a swig of his beer, gurgled it, and then swallowed with a satisfied sigh. He repeated this process two more times before focusing his cold, dead eyes on Malaki.

"What'll it take to make it worth your while? You want money?"

Malaki crossed his arms. "What kind of help?"

"Little o' this, little o' that. You ever been to that house up on the hill?"

Malaki shook his head. "No, but I… I'm not scared of it."

"Good, good." The old man's lips parted in a yellow grin. "And also…"

"Yeah?"

"You ever killed something before?"

Malaki sat up straighter, looking around the bar for anybody eavesdropping. It had cleared out a little bit since he first entered, and they were practically conversing in secret, but still he felt wary.

"I… no, I haven't." He furrowed his eyebrows. "I ain't tryin' to get involved in nothing funny. Nothing… weird."

"Oh, it won't be funny. I've got a place I wanna show you," the old man continued. He reached into his pocket and fumbled with something hidden. "But you'll have to come with me."

"Okay, fine." Malaki crossed his arms. "But get me another round first."

The old man cackled and tipped his imaginary hat to the young man. "I like the sound of that deal."

CHAPTER 9
BENJAMIN "CLIFF" WOODS

"How'd you get their address?" Jeremy eyed me skeptically, wrinkling his nose. "Didn't think they gave that out to just anybody."

I chuckled and brandished my phone. "Naomi knows the mom."

"Ah, I see." He clicked his tongue and looked around at Main Street. "How far down is it?"

"Edge of town." I double-checked the address on my phone. "Not sure I've been over there in a while. It's past George's shop."

"No wonder the sheriff went after them. They must live a few blocks down from where it happened."

We were passing by the section of Main Street with all of the stores and a smattering of restaurants. There weren't as many people as usual, probably due to the thick, gray clouds hanging over the town. It looked like any minute they'd unleash torrents of rain on us. The entire day, they'd blocked out much of the sunlight, giving New Haven an eerie, quiet atmosphere. Cold air blew in, dropping the temperature by double digits from yesterday and assuring us all that a storm was brewing right over our heads.

Jeremy and I weren't eager for the mission we'd been set on, but it felt like the right thing to do. After my conversation with Naomi and her revelations about the sheriff, I felt more confident than ever he *would* try something. People around here were clamoring for answers. If he could pin the tragedy on a new family who'd just moved into town, it would make his life a hell of a lot easier.

When I told Jeremy about Naomi's stance, he actually agreed with her, to my surprise. "Wheeler's always been a dick," he said, reminding me how in middle school he would always throw rocks at the fattest kid in our class. It seemed the man had a reputation and I was the one who'd been ignorant of it.

"You think he'd really try to frame the Dawes?" I asked as we made our way down the sidewalk.

"When he's desperate enough, sure." Jeremy stared up ahead of us, where George's store had once been. "People here, they're already talking about the oldest Dawes kid. They say some awful, nasty stuff, too."

"Naomi said the church women are really worried for Smith. They keep praying for him," I added. "He's having trouble fitting in or something."

He sighed and shook his head. "Sometimes you forget how backward this town can be. Friendliest place to live... unless you're new blood."

George's store had once been a bustling, colorful place in the center of Main Street. Outside, there were always pinwheels hanging from the walls and wind chimes on the edges of his building. Now, all that remained were charred bricks, a pile of rubble in the center of a vacant square. There were no crowds around the scene anymore. They'd moved on to preparing a funeral, comforting George's widow, grieving the young boy lost in the fire. But there were still flowers, Bibles, and handwritten notes piled on the sidewalk, arranged around a framed photograph of George, his wife, and his son. The scene almost brought tears, so I averted my gaze and took a deep breath. It was the first time I'd seen it up close. I couldn't imagine being here the day it happened.

"Still can't believe it sometimes," Jeremy muttered. He had also been looking at the colorful memorial. I saw his jaw trembling under that bushy beard and wondered how he'd kept it together since that day. "I saw him the day before it happened, too. Fucking sad, man.

"It really is."

Jeremy huffed. "I understand people are angry... sure. But why should we tear apart another family? How does that fix anything? How is it fair?"

He shook his head and we carried along in silence after that. The tragedy faded behind us and we each took a few minutes to prepare for the task.

Seeking out the Dawes family was a bold move. The mom had never spoken to either of us before. I wished that Naomi could've come on this trip, but I didn't wanna bother her with it. She was at home with the kids, still resting from the wild events two evenings ago. She was tougher than me, but she still deserved some time to recover from all that. And besides, Jeremy wanted to stay involved with all of this.

I *desperately* needed his support if we really did go up against the sheriff. Only Jeremy — owner of the most farmland in New Haven, from one of the oldest families in New Haven — could go head-to-head with Sheriff Wheeler and be okay.

"How much should we tell Anne?" asked Jeremy, turning to

face me. "Do we wanna be honest or… try not to scare her?"

I fidgeted with my chin hairs, frowning. "We don't even know if the sheriff's going after 'em yet."

Jeremy wore a skeptical look, the same one he'd given me when I told him about my conversation with Naomi. No, I *hadn't* been totally honest with her. I didn't mention anything the sheriff said about watching out for "strangers" or his vague threats. And Jeremy caught on to my deception rather quickly. Rather than call me out on it, he always offered that disapproving, unconvinced stare.

"So, take it easy on her?" he said.

I nodded. "I think that's best for now."

He smirked and stuffed both hands into the pockets of his jeans. "You keep saying that about stuff. What about when it's time to stop putting things off for later?"

"Don't wanna think about it, honestly."

As we reached one of the side street intersections, we had to pause for two large trucks to pull out onto the main road. Jeremy waved to the drivers, who I didn't recognize. One of them rolled down the window to chat with him. The smell of their exhaust met my nose as they idled in place for a minute.

While they conversed, I glanced around at Main Street. The crowd had grown even sparser now. Most of the shops were closing up early, it appeared, except for the weapons store across the road. As I turned my attention to it, I recognized Malaki Banks, his slicked-back hair a standout in New Haven. He usually roamed around with a don't-care, chest-out stance, but today he was crouched, lurking close to the buildings. As I watched, Malaki snapped his head in either direction, then darted into the weapons store as fast as possible. The door shut behind him, and I looked away, confused.

"You coming?" Jeremy asked.

I noticed the two big trucks were gone now. We crossed the side street, and as we did I told him what I'd seen.

"That kid ain't up to anything good. Never is," Jeremy growled, casting his own look back at the weapons store. He narrowed his eyes. "Damn idiot's gonna hurt somebody if he keeps up. Maybe himself."

Changing the subject, I said, "I think it's two blocks up here." I pointed straight ahead of us, where a small house was coming into view. "Not far from George's shop, really."

Jeremy took his hands out of his pockets and checked his phone. "Almost seven. You think they're home?"

"I'd guess so. They had baseball practice today, but that ended half an hour ago." I gritted my teeth and tried to fight against the nervous feeling that had blossomed in my stomach. "She and all the kids should be there."

"What's our plan, exactly?" Jeremy glanced upward at the sky, then to the house looming closer. "Should we ask for an alibi or anything?"

"They were at the game, Jeremy. Let's just play it easy, say we're checking on them since they're new. Maybe ask how the kids are liking the town?" I cringed visibly and realized just how unprepared we were. "We could stand out here and plan something if you want?"

Jeremy chuckled and rubbed his forehead. "We're gonna get drenched out here in a few minutes or look like idiots in there. Let's just go for it. It's what we came here to do."

The house was tiny, on the very edge of Main Street. Only twenty yards past it, New Haven's cracking sidewalks and four-lane street disappeared, replaced by a winding country road, endless stalks of corn. Pretty soon, they would double in height, and the house itself would feel even smaller.

A single-story, white structure, with a decrepit-looking roof and a yard that had grown for weeks on end—that grass looked awfully similar to my hair in the mornings. There were weeds reaching up the sides of the house, veins growing in the gutters and down the walls. Every exterior surface had chipped and faded paint. The building might've been empty if not for the blue minivan parked next to the sidewalk. By comparison to the house, the van looked pretty nice now.

Without a word, Jeremy and I passed by the vehicle and approached the front door of the house. The cement porch, standing only a foot high, was scattered with children's toys and a few pieces of broken furniture. Two baseballs and a single bat were tucked away into the corner, as well as a battered glove. They must've been Smith's. I didn't realize the kid lacked a backpack to carry them in. I could've easily brought him one if I'd known.

See, this is why I need Naomi's help with this stuff.

Jeremy stepped to the front door and knocked three times, sharp raps with his knuckles. I held my breath, wondering if anybody would answer. It struck me how much cowardice it'd take to try and blame this family, this single mom, for the attack on George's. No matter how much pain had been caused in that fire, or how peculiar the oldest kid seemed, it wouldn't do any good to blame it on these people. They were just trying to get by, not to hurt anyone.

The door swung open and Anne Dawes looked out with wide, terrified eyes. She wore her hair in a bun, and two young children were clinging to her hands.

"Ms. Dawes?" Jeremy asked.

"What do you want?" she hissed, glancing from Jeremy to

me like a deer in the headlights.

"We just need to talk for a few minutes." Jeremy fidgeted with the bottom of his shirt, casting a hopeless look in my direction. He refocused on Anne. "Is that okay?"

"But why?" Her voice was frail. I noticed her arms were terribly thin and shaking.

"We wanna help you, Ms. Dawes," I said, stepping in front of Jeremy and trying to move him backward. If we both stood right up against her, she'd only get more frightened. "Just let us explain ourselves, okay? Then we'll leave. I swear."

Anne Dawes' eyes pierced mine. They were bright and full of passion, but not trust. Then, to my shock, she took a few steps backward. The kids at either side of her did the same, gazing up at me with intense fear. They hadn't spoken, had barely moved, but I knew what they were thinking.

All of the Dawes acted as if we were coming to take them away. I wondered if we'd been too late, if the sheriff or somebody had already come by to threaten them. Worse yet, I didn't know if they'd admit it. This meeting might've been for nothing.

"In here." Anne led the way into a small room on the right. She ushered the two kids inside and then stood at the entrance, watching me and Jeremy traipse into the house. I tried to look over her shoulder and get a better view of the other rooms, but Anne glared at me until I lowered my head and obediently slumped into the room she'd indicated.

Everywhere I could see, the house was carpeted, though chunks of it were loose and it hadn't been glued down properly by the walls. I glimpsed the kitchen and what looked like a bedroom. Both were dark, the windows blocked by heavy curtains, deep shadows in the corners. The kitchen had grimy dishes all over, an overspilling trash bag in the center of the floor.

The other room had a single twin bed, as well as a rocking chair. Both were in poor shape, and I couldn't see anything else.

"This is weird," I whispered to Jeremy as we entered the sitting room.

He didn't answer. His eyes were roaming the area, locking on the two children who sat with their backs against one wall. The little girl had a red ball, and she was tossing it in the air and catching it, a pitiful smile on her face.

There was a single couch in this room. One end of it had fluff leaking out and a nasty, charred area on the armrest. Behind it, the wall was entirely blank except for a single photograph; it looked like a family portrait. I tried to get a better look, but once again, Anne stepped between me and it. I felt her hand on my back, ushering me toward the couch, and then she quickly started talking.

"You two sit, there ya go. Kids! Get out of here." She swatted at them with her hand, and the kids started giggling, scampering into the other room like mice. "These kids, outta control."

Jeremy and I awkwardly took a seat on one side of the couch, trying to stay away from the blackened armrest and slashed cushion. We situated ourselves, pressed closer together than either of us liked, and faced Anne Dawes. She had seated herself in a wooden chair in front of a brick fireplace. As I expected, there were bricks missing from it and the interior was rough, like it hadn't seen a true fire in years. There were cobwebs in the corners, a trail of slime leading up toward the ceiling, and children's toys scattered on the ground. I noticed a blue truck that looked curiously like mine. The front of it was smashed.

After a moment, Jeremy began, "So, Ms. Dawes—"

"Smith!" she interrupted him, screaming the name.

I heard scurrying from the doorway the two kids had gone

through. When I looked, I saw it led straight into the kitchen, and I could make out one edge of the same table from earlier. Smith appeared, his eyes wide and petrified, but he stepped into the sitting room anyway. He wore a bulky set of headphones and his baseball shirt, though with athletic shorts on now.

"Come in here," Anne commanded him, gesturing to the floor beside her chair. "Take those off."

Without questioning, Smith hunched over, pulled down the headphones, and took a seat with his back to the brick fireplace. He peered up at Jeremy and myself. At first, he refused to look at us directly. Then I made eye contact with him for just a moment, and he never looked away again.

Jeremy hesitated this time, probably wondering if she would interrupt him again, but he finally went on. "Ms. Dawes, how're you, uh... how's New Haven, so far?"

Her gaze was dead as it landed on Jeremy. I felt him recoil. Her lips parted slightly and she breathed eerily quiet. "It's a nice place for me. The kids have struggled. Lots of... heat."

"Sure has been." Jeremy chuckled, and I could tell he was trying to move the conversation to a more casual place. "You haven't seen one of our big New Haven storms yet, have you?"

Anne Dawes raised an eyebrow. She glanced back at the doorway her kids had gone through, as if listening for something, then returned to Jeremy. "No. No, I haven't."

I looked through that same doorway, ignoring Smith's gaze drilling into my forehead, and saw the other two kids were seated on the kitchen floor. The two of them faced each other, holding hands, sitting with their legs crossed. Neither said a word, and neither blinked. They laughed in silence, never looking away.

"And do you all need anything? Any food or... supplies?"

Jeremy cleared his throat, said, "excuse me," and coughed for a minute. Anne seemed to find this amusing. He reoriented himself and went on. "I've got a nice crop this year. Could bring you all some corn or some fruit, whatever your kids'll eat."

"My kids will eat anything." Anne moved her piercing gaze from Jeremy to me. "Smith likes you."

I stumbled over the words I'd prepared. Both of them were staring at me now, neither blinking. Anne started scratching at her arm, hard enough to break the skin. Her expression didn't change, but she continued clawing at her forearm, hardly more than bone and skin.

"I can bring you a…" I focused on Smith, trying not to let her distract me or break my train of thought. "A backpack, you know? To keep your baseball stuff in. And a glove if you want? My son's on your team." When he didn't answer, I added, "Would you want them?"

Smith narrowed his eyes. In a voice like his mother's, he hissed, "Are you like the other men? They said —"

Anne snapped her head in that direction so quickly it made me jump. He instantly shut up. She glared at him until Smith cowered backward, bringing his knees to his chest and staring at the ground.

When I spoke next, I directed it to both of them. I wanted to reach out and console the boy, but there was no telling what Anne might've done. "No, we aren't like the other men. I don't know…" I looked to Jeremy for support and tried to ignore Anne's constant scratching. Her skin had turned a shade of red now, and her mouth hung open slightly. "I don't know who came here to talk to you, but we aren't like them. We want to *help* you. I know… I know you haven't done anything wrong." Now I focused on Anne mostly, leaning forward slightly and dropping my voice. "You're just here for a fresh start, right? We want to help you. Protect you."

Smith gazed at me, longingly, his lips stuck in a perpetual frown. Anne, however, was colder. Her hands were shaking wildly now and she dropped them to her knees. I saw a trickle of blood running down her arm from the site she'd been clawing at.

"We are *fine*," Anne said, sitting rigid in her chair. Jeremy tensed beside me as her eyes shone with fire. "We have help from the church women. Like Susan and Naomi. We don't need you *men*."

I thought about mentioning that Naomi was my wife, since I knew they'd had interactions before, but I decided against it. Her disapproval of me might outweigh her affection for my wife, and I didn't want to throw a wrench in that relationship. Not when it was just beginning. Better to let Naomi work her magic and keep us separate in Anne's mind.

Jeremy drew out his phone and Anne stiffened, not moving a muscle. He put up his hands defensively, letting the device fall to his lap. "Will you take our numbers, at least? Just in case anyone comes by. Any... of those men. We just want to know if they do, so we can help you."

Before Anne could protest, I jumped in. "Like I said, we believe you, and we trust you."

"You don't know anything about us," Anne said. She reached for Smith and shoved him toward the doorway. "Get outta here, you."

Smith lumbered to his feet and slunk out of the room. As he passed through the doorway, he turned around and looked at me one last time. He offered a gentle, feeble wave. I smiled in return. Then the boy reached down for his two siblings and led them into the depths of the house, out of my view. —I wondered what, exactly, was back there, but I didn't dare ask.

With the children all gone, Anne's exterior became even harder. She stood from the chair and scowled at the two of us, hands on her bony hips. "My husband was a very bad man. I've dealt with very bad men my entire life. And, you know what?" She spat on the ground at our feet. "I don't think you're any different. I think you're here *pretending,* and I'm sick of pretenders." This last part she added forcefully, whirling around to shove the chair she'd been sitting in. It toppled to the floor.

Jeremy was wide-eyed, glued to the couch. I opened my mouth to speak, but Anne pointed one shaking finger directly at me, and all words evaporated from my tongue. Her fingernail was red with the blood from her arm.

"Get out of here," she snarled, "or I'll kill you, too."

I rose to my feet, hands in the air as if a gun had been drawn. I kicked Jeremy's shin and he followed suit, putting away his phone. As we backed toward the front door, I glanced at the wall behind the couch. To my shock, there was no photograph. Just a blank wall of chipped paint and children's fingerprints.

Anne smirked as Jeremy fumbled with the doorknob. I thought for a brief moment she might've locked it, might be toying with us, but then it unlatched. Jeremy stepped outside first, more shaken than I'd seen him in a long time. I followed, backing outside and into the storm-brewing street, but first I offered one last statement to Anne.

"Please don't be afraid to ask for help," I begged her. I reached inside my pocket, fumbled for my wallet, and extracted a twenty-dollar bill. I let it flutter to the ground as I pulled the door shut. "Believe me. We're on your side, Ms. Dawes."

When we stepped off the porch, neither of us speaking, I heard something slam against the door from the inside. But I didn't look back. Whatever went on in that house, it was better left unquestioned. There were too many other questions turning in my brain already. I didn't need more.

Jeremy and I reached the sidewalk. For a moment, we stood by the minivan and looked back at the house. Small, entrapped with vines, a mess. I wasn't sure how to feel anymore. When we first arrived, I had felt one-hundred percent sure that Anne Dawes was innocent, a victim. And now...

"I don't know what to think about her," I admitted to Jeremy as we hurried away on the sidewalk. It was still a bit of a walk to my truck, and pretty soon the rain would pummel these streets. I felt sure of that, at least.

"She don't want much help o' ours," Jeremy said, chewing on his lip. He was still a few shades paler than when we entered, and his hands were trembling. "Think the sheriff's been by to see her already?"

"Seemed like it. From how she acted." I ground my teeth together and kicked at a rock on the sidewalk. There were even fewer people outside now, just a few stragglers up by the shops. "Let's just keep an eye out for anything else. Maybe the sheriff finds a lead and he'll leave that family alone."

Jeremy blew a raspberry and shrugged. "Don't know what we can do, really. I got a real weird feeling at that house. Kinda like..."

I clasped him on the shoulder. "Let's not worry about it right now. Just get outta this rain."

We started walking faster after that. The wind picked up as we made our way down the sidewalk. Thick, drooping, dark clouds overhead were gathering force and multiplying. Thunder clapped somewhere in the far distance, over the flatlands. It was so dark, I could barely make out the line of hills to our north, barely see the abandoned house, standing so defiantly against the encroaching storms. I didn't want to be outside when those clouds unleashed their fury and smacked these streets with torrents of rain. Truth be told, I didn't want to be anywhere but home.

Jeremy didn't wanna say it, and neither did I. We danced around the subject while we found my truck and I climbed into it. Even as we said goodbye, Jeremy waving from the sidewalk, neither of us mentioned it. But the suspicion had taken hold, creeping up our spines, gripping the back of our heads.

I wasn't certain anymore that Anne Dawes was innocent. And I didn't know how to defend her if she was. Sheriff Wheeler held immense power in New Haven. He knew every trick in the book. If he wanted, he could turn the entire town against the Dawes, drive them out of here or — even worse — toss Anne in jail. If I tried to defend her, it might be me.

As sporadic, fat raindrops splattered my windshield, I had no doubt that another storm was amassing. One of these days, a reckoning would come. George's death ensured it. Somebody would feel the sheriff's wrath.

And maybe it should be her, rather than me.

CHAPTER 10
IN NEW HAVEN

Jeremy Adams trudged along Main Street, heading for the police station. Both hands shoved into his pockets, the bearded veteran farmer made his way through town alone, keeping his head down. Cliff's truck had disappeared into the distance only minutes earlier, and now Jeremy trekked toward the station, where he knew Sheriff Wheeler would be.

Even if Anne Dawes was threatening, and even if she *acted* guilty, he didn't for a moment think about turning on her. Sheriff Wheeler had prejudice bubbling up to his eyeballs, and Jeremy didn't believe in letting that kind of thing go untested. If she turned out to be guilty, then fine, but not until the sheriff played by the book, followed the right process. If he knew anything about the Wheeler family, it was they didn't tend to follow the same rules as everyone else.

A fat raindrop smacked his shoulder, his cheek. Jeremy groaned and picked up his pace.

"Miserable day to do all this," he muttered to himself.

The police station was still a few blocks away. Even if he got in and out quickly — said his piece to the sheriff, hurried away — he'd get caught in the storm.

Jeremy glanced across Main Street, saw the dusty sideroad leading to the baseball field. On one side of that offshoot, barely more than an alley, there was a sports bar and on the other a boutique. The shop looked like it'd closed down for the day, but the sports bar was humming. A few televisions flickered inside, and he saw someone familiar exiting the main door.

Malaki.

That kid's not even old enough to drink, Jeremy huffed. He stood, with his arms crossed, waiting for the boy to make eye contact. But Malaki ducked his head and hurried along the sidewalk, heading the same direction Jeremy needed to go.

Jeremy moved slowly, on his own side of the road, keeping an eye on the boy from across the street. Malaki tapped at his phone for a moment and then stuffed it away. He reached for something else in his pocket and pulled it out. Jeremy couldn't see from his vantage point what the boy was holding, but Malaki studied it intently.

The boy turned to peer up and down the street, scowling. His eyes roamed the sidewalks frantically, until they met Jeremy's.

Jeremy glanced down and saw what he was holding.

In his hands, Malaki held a sleek pistol.

He yelled out, "Hey, kid!" and stepped off the sidewalk. *I'm gonna confront that kid,* he thought to himself, but too late.

Malaki darted to the right, into an alleyway. He cut away from the road, brandishing his weapon, and took off at a jog. Heading away from Main Street, past the baseball field, toward the hills.

Jeremy crossed the road anyway and watched as the figure moved into the darkness between buildings. He vanished into the haze of rain and shadows, but Jeremy had a feeling he'd kept going. Toward those hills, north of town.

He knew — from stories his dad told him before he passed away — that there used to be a trail leading up those hills. It ran from New Haven, beside the baseball field, up to the abandoned house. Back when the Donnellys still lived there, they used the trail to come into town. After they died, there were rumors of a cult using the house, even coming down on that very trail. The stories were never specific, Jeremy knew, just like the strange rumors about that family's death, and they were never proven. But a part of him felt like they *were* true, at least some of them.

Jeremy stood on the sidewalk, two blocks from the station, and watched those hills in the distance, storm clouds rolling over them. The trail was overgrown and nearly impossible to find now.

He remembered the impending thunderstorm and pushed away his rambling thoughts. But he couldn't shake the image of Malaki's face as he'd darted into the alley. The gun in his hands. He shivered.

"Something else to warn the sheriff about," he mumbled.

Not that it mattered. This whole trip was a waste of time, and he knew it. Even if he *heard* Malaki confess to starting the fire and told the sheriff so, it wouldn't matter. Sheriff Wheeler wasn't gonna contest Malaki, one of the few high school graduates who stuck around. He wouldn't turn against a New Haven local like that.

He had his sights on someone else. Anyone else. He needed someone to blame, and by some misfortune the Dawes had stepped right into his crossfire.

Jeremy made his way to the police station hesitantly, trying to piece together what defense he could use. He could try to reason with the sheriff, but logic didn't mean much when hysteria took over. If nothing else, he'd try to slow the sheriff's witch hunt and force him to consider other suspects.

"Here goes nothing," Jeremy said, heading for the door.

Behind the police station, perched in the hills, the abandoned house stared down. Jeremy tried not to think about it or what Malaki could be doing up there.

CHAPTER 11
NAOMI WOODS

I was in my usual spot on the back porch, beside the table. It was sweltering outside, and a sweating glass of lemonade sat to my right. Across from me, Kaia was leaning forward, entranced in another book. I'd never been much of a reader, but she devoured words like nobody else around here. I smiled at the sight and refocused on the view from our porch.

She's really gonna be something. I felt pride swelling in me, hopefulness. I was so lucky to have a daughter like her, to be the mother of someone who gave me so much hope, who imbued so much love into the world.

We could sit like this for hours if the day allowed it. Kaia would often sink into a book, just like that, and not say a word for thirty minutes. I preferred the view from our porch over a page full of words, and in a similar way I would sink into it.

Moments like this, I could be totally calm and savor the energy around us, the connection with the land. From my seat, staring past the big oak tree, I could make out most of Cliff's farmland. Back here, it was soybeans and mostly corn. It marked the seasons, as the green stalks peeked out from the earth and then grew taller. Birds overhead chirped to themselves with the rustling of the trees. I tried to soak in every little detail of the natural world, allowing it to cover me. It was like a sort of therapy.

I'd have loved to walk among those trees, on forgotten forest trails, instead of just looking at them. But the clouds overhead warned us to stay near shelter. — Anyway, my legs were still painfully sore from the bike ride.

If it did rain, I could sit here on the porch, dry, and welcome it. The heat had been constant, Cliff said the crops were struggling, and maybe some rain would help. More than anything, I enjoyed the sound of rain, the way a storm pulsed in the air. Sitting on this porch, watching a heavy storm roll in and unleash... few things made me happier and calmer.

The porch itself was fairly typical: a coat of dark red over the wood, which Cliff and I had painted years ago. The floorboards were starting to lose their color as it chipped away, bit by bit. But that was to be expected when a porch got so much use. Besides the table where I sat, we had a bench swing hanging by two small chains, two antique stools, a collection of flowers and plants, a rattling ceiling fan right above me, and a small dinner bell I'd inherited from my own home.

Just off the porch, Cliff had his grill (sitting unused for weeks under a tarp) and a pile of chopped wood. There was a large oak tree about twenty feet away. Once, there had been a play place beside it, until the kids stopped using it and the plastic became moldy and discolored. Cliff's farm equipment and other junk—a five-gallon bucket, propane tanks, a tool chest—would migrate to the porch and then disappear when I got after him. Then it would return, and the cycle continued. Otherwise, this backyard had been the exact same ever since we moved in twenty years ago.

I picked up my glass of lemonade and sipped it. Hard to

believe it'd been twenty years. Scanning the fields, I settled on the distant forest of oaks and hickory trees. The same view I'd been mesmerized by for two decades. There were birds circling the treetops, almost too small to see from this distance. The leaves were turning over, as they say. Each individual one quivered as the wind picked up. The whole canopy swayed in unison, rustling sounds carrying all the way across the field to me.

I could see myself out there, among those towering, dancing trees. Holding Kaia's hand, back when it was much smaller. For hours, the two of us had explored the untamed wilderness, as I pointed out interesting features in the tree bark or named the type based on their leaves. Oak trees, hickory, a smattering of maples. Kaia didn't care much for the names, but she marveled at the size and beauty.

There were animals sometimes, deer in the distance or squirrels dangling their tails so close we could've touched them. Kaia always had such a fascination with the forest. Not just the vegetation or the animals but all of it together, the whole ecosystem. When she and Nathaniel started to venture out on their own, I didn't worry too much. By the time she was a teenager, Kaia knew the landscape better than me, and she *understood* it. She could hold her own in any situation. That fact never changed about her.

I placed my glass back on the table and glanced in her direction. "You're still planning on environmental science, right?" I asked, breaking the quiet fog.

Kaia looked up from her pages. "Yeah, Mom. Not gonna change." She frowned, set the open book on the table. "Did I tell you? I got a letter again. In-state this time."

I grinned, nodding my approval. "That's great, baby. What is that, a dozen acceptances?"

Kaia laughed and rolled her eyes. "No, Mom, not a dozen. Doesn't matter anyway. I dunno where I'm going. Almost everyone from school does."

With a knowing smile, I put my hands together and said, "Kaia, you're so smart. You're gorgeous, determined... you won't have any problems, wherever you choose. Whichever college *you* pick, they'll gain an amazing environmental scientist. So don't even worry. *You're* in charge here. You still have a couple months, really."

"Thanks, Mom." Kaia turned away as she blushed. She swept her eyes over the landscape and I got the feeling she wanted to say more. Instead, she reached for the book and cast herself into its pages. Her expression looked far away.

I did wonder where she'd end up. It wasn't an easy decision. Hadn't been for me and definitely not for someone like Kaia, who'd never lived outside of New Haven. She was already too big for this town, too ambitious. There was a whole world out there she'd never experienced, waiting for her. Cliff was the same way when he went to college, but without the ambition.

I fought the urge to dive into that sweet memory and focused on the present. On my daughter. *Mindfulness,* I remembered. Things were changing fast. I needed to appreciate this while I had it. We were barreling into the future, full speed ahead. Twenty years had flown by, and not a single year more was ever guaranteed.

"I'm goin' out with Allison in a bit," Kaia said, still staring down into her book. "I've been tryin' to see her for a while. Found time, finally."

"You worried for her still?"

I remembered one of our conversations a week ago, before the wedding. Kaia had been on edge about the whole thing, concerned about Malaki's nature. I couldn't blame her, though I didn't know the young man very well. From what she told me and what I'd seen of him, he wasn't the kind of boy I wanted my kids associated with.

She nodded, not meeting my eyes. I doubted she was still reading. "Malaki's been... acting weird. More than normal."

"He still drives that red convertible, right?"

Kaia nodded, eyebrows raised. "Yeah, why?"

I batted away the question. "Couldn't remember. I think you should just be honest with her," I went on. "Tell her you're worried. Maybe she can explain things. You two are good friends. I'm sure she'll appreciate it."

"Yeah, maybe so." Kaia chewed on her lip. "I guess I'll try to."

"Just don't get caught in the storm, okay?" I advised her. "Supposed to be rough tonight."

She agreed and returned to her novel. At least, she pretended to.

The truth was, I'd asked about Malaki's car because Susan from church told me something unnerving a few days before. She'd been seeing a car fitting that description driving up to the abandoned house a few times. It might be nothing; Malaki was a stupid teenager, even though he'd graduated high school now. But it didn't make me feel any better about the whole situation. Things would never calm down if you had idiots like Malaki poking around where they shouldn't.

The screen door behind us swung open with a creak and Nathaniel emerged. As he stepped outside, it slapped back against the frame. His scrawny torso was still dripping from his shower. He carried an empty glass and made straight for the lemonade pitcher between us.

"How was practice?" I asked as he filled his cup, more than happy for a distraction from my anxious thoughts.

Nathaniel pulled out a chair between the two of us and sat, elbows resting on the table. "Eh, alright. I was tired today."

Kaia rolled her eyes and murmured something under her breath about "video games."

I gestured at the view ahead of us and looked from her to Nathaniel. "I'd say we should go for a walk but it might storm soon."

"And tomorrow, too," Kaia added.

"This weekend, maybe?" Nathaniel suggested. He took a long drink from his lemonade, his eyes set on me.

"Maybe, we'll see." I fidgeted with my shorts and forced myself to meet his gaze. "Was Smith at baseball today?"

He nodded, taking another drink. "Yeah. He actually talked to me."

Kaia looked up for a second and made eye contact with me, but I couldn't read her expression. Something inquisitive.

Nathaniel continued, "Hey, Mom, about that... Can I ask you something?"

"Of course."

"This kid at practice..." Nathaniel rubbed the top of his head, sending water droplets onto the table and porch. Kaia inched away from him. "It was last week, I think. This kid said it about that... that abandoned house. The people who used to live there. And I dunno if it's true or not. I thought you might."

I frowned thoughtfully. I had an idea where this conversation was headed. I'd dealt with New Haven townies and their opinions about that house for years. "What'd he say?" *Or, more likely, what did his parents tell him?*

Kaia was fully invested in the conversation, now. She hadn't closed her book or set it on the table, but she glanced from Nathaniel to me. We both waited for his response, to hear exactly what kind of rumors the kid at baseball had spread. —I knew the cruel nature of middle schoolers, and I knew that it played into the legend of that house. Everybody in town had grown up under its shadowing, swapping myths and stories like trading cards. It didn't surprise me anymore, and I couldn't stop it from happening. But I didn't want Nathaniel to think like that. Especially not now.

"Well, the kid…" Nathaniel rubbed his head again. He paused. "He said that house was full of freaks, you know, ever since it was built. Weird people, creepy people. And that they haunt it, now, because they all died."

I took a deep breath before answering. Kaia raised her eyebrows at me. She'd probably heard the same type of rumor in middle school, already knew my response. I didn't need to worry about her sinking into any sort of prejudiced mindset.

"No, Nate, that's… not true." I offered him a warm smile. "I think you already guessed that, though. Do you wanna know the *truth* about that house?"

He nodded quickly.

"That house… The family who lived there were called the Donnellys. Your dad knows more about them than me, but… I know our town should've done more to help them. We let them down, you know. They deserved better. And now that house is old, falling apart, and… and there are bad things inside of it, yes, but we're the ones to blame. New Haven." I dropped my gaze, staring at the boards under the table. "And whatever happens with that, there's nobody to blame. This town should've done more."

"But what happened to the Donn… the people who used to live there?" Nathaniel persisted. He glanced at Kaia now, too. Maybe he'd figured out she knew some of that dark history from me. "Did they die?"

Such a simple, cold question. I sighed and adjusted my shoulders. "They did. Years before I even came here." I added, "But it doesn't mean they're all the way gone."

"Don't believe everything you hear in town," Kaia said, directing her warning to Nathaniel. She shrugged one shoulder and glanced at me for support. I nodded. "Most people there don't understand."

I recognized that phrase from a conversation we'd had on our own and couldn't help but chuckle. She was more like me every day, in both good and bad ways. Her interests might be different, but a lot of them stemmed from the same root as mine. I wondered for a moment if I'd been wrong about something. Maybe Nathaniel wasn't the one I should worry about. He was young and curious but not always brave.

Kaia. She was brave. And she had as much of a fascination with that house as I did. It was something to keep an eye on. Something to think on.

"How's Smith been doing at practice?" I asked Nathaniel, trying not to sound overly interested. He probably found it weird that I asked about Smith so often, but he was my best source of information for this.

"He's fine." Nathaniel hesitated, tapping his fingers on his lemonade glass. "I think he's starting to not like baseball, though. The… the other kids aren't very nice to him."

"Oh, that's not good. Do you stand up for him?"

"I try to." Nathaniel huffed. "It's hard, though. 'Cause some of them are my friends, too. But they… say stuff to him, and I can tell it hurts him."

"Don't be afraid to tell them to shut up," Kaia interjected. She was gazing into her pages still, speaking with the lazy tone of someone who isn't at all affected by the situation. "Middle school friends don't even last."

"You're still friends with Allison."

"Yeah, but that's only one." She rolled her eyes. "Trust me, Nate, I would know. I'm older than you."

"Whatever."

The conversation devolved into silence again. I didn't know what to say to all that. Why did I even ask about Smith if I wasn't gonna tackle the subject head-on? Yes, he was different from the other kids. And it was bold of him to even join the baseball team, but I wanted it to work out for him *so badly*. I wanted him to love this town, these people. And I wanted them to accept him for the kind-hearted, intelligent kid he was. But nobody, it seemed, wanted to look past his physical limitations or the label of "Outsider."

Nathaniel seemed content for now. Kaia was enveloped by her book.

I thought we'd find a better time for that discussion in the future. I didn't have the energy to dive into that complicated subject, not right now. It felt better to just exist with the two of them. I got to staring around again, noticed my plants needed watering, the distant birds were few now, Cliff's toolbox had once again found its way next to my trailing clematis at the edge of the deck. The bugs were particularly annoying in the evenings, always flies buzzing in my ears or mosquitoes landing on my arms.

I shook these concerns away and tried to focus on my kids. It wasn't very often we were all three together now. Even rarer that Cliff joined. Not with everything going on.

While Kaia read her novel, Nathaniel stared into the far distance with me, both of us eyeing the tree line across the fields.

I wondered who would speak first. Who would break this peacefulness.

"Can you tell me a story, Mom?" He asked the question without glancing at me, sipping on the last of his lemonade. "About before you met Dad? When you rode around in those hippie vans and stuff?"

I reached out and touched the back of his head, smiling. "Not right now, baby. I'm too tired. A different time I will. I promise."

He accepted this answer and downed the last of his lemonade. "That's okay. I'm tired too."

He stood from the table, said his goodbyes, and vanished into the house. As the screen door smacked shut, I wondered if I'd made a mistake. He'd wanted to stay out here, hadn't he? He'd been searching for a reason to sit with me and talk. Perhaps I should've been more thoughtful or given him something small to think on. A small story. I could've offered that. But I didn't.

Kaia mumbled something about "video games" and clearly wasn't lost in thought like myself. I looked at her for a minute as she continued reading and then reached for the pitcher to fill up my glass once more.

While I drank my second helping of lemonade, Kaia closed her book for the final time and left the table. She ran inside to change, we said quick goodbyes, and then she started walking down the driveway, waiting for Allison. I didn't know where she was going or when she'd be back, but all of a sudden I found myself alone on the porch.

Instinct took over and I glanced at the hillside in the far distance. Those aggressive, sloping roofs stared down at me. And it happened all at once. The way it used to. One moment, I was sitting on the porch, drinking lemonade. Then I dropped it. Glass shattered on the ground next to me. Broken glass glinting in the sunlight. My eyes closed, darkness overtook me. Vivid, visceral images rushing back. Smells and sounds I'd tried so hard to forget.

Unexplainable. Unpredictable. The flashbacks consumed me, and I was drowning in them, with nobody to save me.

<> <> <>

I am in the darkest hallway I have ever known. There are walls to either side of me but covered in slime and mold. The floorboards creak with every tentative step I take, threatening to give out, to break entirely. I stumble forward, throwing my arms out, searching for anything stable. There is only air, stale and cold, like it has never seen the sun. Fungus lingers on either side of me. I shiver and try not to lose hope. I have to find a way out of here.

The walls are horribly gross, but I need to orient myself. I put a hand out and wince as I touch something squirming, vile. I move forward again, into the pitch darkness. I can't even see my own arms. I can't see anything in any direction. What's standing directly in front of me or crouching in the hallway behind. There is nothing. There is only darkness and fear.

This haunted house is filled with much more than ghosts.

I hear something beside me, behind the walls. Inside them. It follows me as I limp ahead, wincing, hoping this is the way. There's no telling whether I'm going deeper into the house or toward the exit. I'm not sure if there is an exit anymore. But I press on, trying not to scream, trying not to let it hear me. The moaning floor gives me away. Whatever is crawling in those walls, it stays right next to me. It will never leave.

"Oh, God." I cover my mouth with a hand, whimpering.

The noise is getting louder. It's scratching at the wall now. I can hear it moving up and down, only a foot away from me, only the fragile barrier between us. I decide to stand still, hoping it will move past me. But that's a terrible mistake.

My senses are hyperactive. I can feel it beside me. I can sense its presence. Those long nails move faster and faster, almost digging at the wood. I bite my lip to stop from screaming. There is no other sound now that I've stopped moving. Only it. Only my shallow breaths.

With a thunderous crash, it breaks through the wall. I lurch away from it, fall to the ground. My knee scrapes on the wood and bleeds, drips. My flesh is torn away, splinters dig into my leg. I cry out in pain and feel it grip my ankle. Those long nails are digging into flesh, crawling up my calf, to my thigh. Such a strong grip. I'm struggling, kicking, yelling for anyone to help me. But that, too, is a mistake.

The entire house is alive now. It moves and taunts me. The creature from the wall is dragging me into its darkness. I dig my nails into the floor, trying anything to fight against it. But nothing works. It has me in its grip. As I cast one last look down the hallway, I see a light at the very end. Feeble and shaky, but there, somewhere.

Then the creature yanks and I'm thrashed against the floor. My head smacks it, my vision dims, and he's drawing me toward him. I can't fight any longer. I bleed away.

PART 2
ENTERING

CHAPTER 1
KAIA WOODS

"How has it been so many years?" Allison grabbed a pinecone from the grass beside us and stared at it for a moment. "Feels like just last week we came here... but it's been almost two years, hasn't it?"

I tried to pinpoint exactly when we'd stopped coming here, when the fast-moving cars and rush of noise from the interstate no longer appealed to us. But I couldn't remember a specific time or moment. It was like a relationship that slowly faded into nothing. It almost hurt worse to realize I couldn't remember than to think about how long ago it'd been.

"Something like that, yeah." I pulled at blades of grass between my legs, brushing my fingers along their abrasive and smooth edges.

"Time just goes so quick, ya know?" Allison shook her head, mesmerized. "And now I'm married! I mean... Jesus Christ, it's weird. Growing up."

I looked at her, smiling, and then down at the cars below us. The interstate had a life of its own, a constant drone of engines. In my mind, it was the fastest place on earth. Those people were racing, though not against each other. They were racing against time. It was a joy to watch them, as time stood still for us. Like it had in early high school, when we came here after school.

From this hillside, we stared down at the people careening past and at the exit ramp, which nobody ever took. Of all the afternoons and evenings here, I only saw a car merge onto that incline maybe a dozen times. Once they reached the top, *nobody* turned left and crossed the overpass. They always went right, straight to the gas station or Dairy Queen. (The only two buildings out here.) And then directly back to the interstate. To drive to New Haven, on the left, was unthinkable.

That fast food restaurant held memories of its own. It had been our spot for our freshman and sophomore years. And the overpass next to it. You could actually stroll onto the road there, which — like I said — never had any traffic, and feel the interstate shaking the ground. Smell the fumes and peer down, over the side, as hundreds of beasts swarmed past. They reminded me of buffalo stampedes in a way. Best viewed from that overpass, a safe place. Or from our hillside.

"Remember when we used to throw stuff down there?" I asked Allison, chuckling at the memory. "Like those eggs?"

Allison fell onto her back, laughing hysterically. She stared up at the sky, truly beautiful, grown up, married. Best not to think about her asshole husband.

"I forgot about those. Your idea, right?"

I shrugged and felt radiant. "I mean, who else?"

"Do you remember that one truck?" Allison's eyes were closed now as she leaned back. She was so pale, especially with an overcast sky blocking all sunlight. She'd lost weight over the past few months. I wondered if she was getting sick, if she was struggling with anxiety again, if she couldn't sleep at her new house.

As she recounted the story—how we'd actually hit one redneck's truck with an egg and gotten yolk all over the side of his vehicle—I replayed those images in my mind.

How we snuck halfway down this hill and tossed eggs into the traffic below, scurrying back up to the tree line anytime we thought someone might've seen us. Our plan was simple: throw eggs at the nearest lane, so they couldn't take the exit and hunt us down. Still worried us, though, whenever someone would glare in our direction or switch on their turn signal. That's what hiding at the edge of the forest was for.

"We didn't *hurt* anyone," I reminded her. "Most of them eggs just hit the ground."

"We could've though." She smiled mischievously. "We were pretty badass teenagers."

I rolled my eyes, now stretching out on the grass beside her. "That's what *every* teen says, Allison."

There was a moment's pause. I remembered something and groaned loudly, smacking myself in the forehead.

"What, Kaia?"

"I forgot that necklace I was gonna give you." I pounded a fist into the grass. "Damn it, I had it on my dresser and everything."

"Oh, I'm sorry." She frowned. "You can give it to me next time we hang out."

"Yeah, true."

"Maybe we can go to town again and I'll buy that hippie hoodie from the crystal store."

"Oh, yeah. Good idea." I smirked. She rarely ever went to that place willingly. "Even if Ms. Hargrave tries to give you a reading, again?"

"Hey, it's worth it for the hoodie."

Silence overtook us now. We lay together, shoulder-to-shoulder, peering up at a gray ceiling of accumulation. I held up my hand, watching as an ant crawled into the valley between my fingers. I felt Allison's eyes on me, her breathing slow, almost mute. Any moment now, those clouds would unleash on us. We were probably a five-minute walk from the car, parked over by the Dairy Queen, and another twenty minutes from there to my house. But I didn't want to move from this spot. I didn't want to let her go.

"We need to hang more," I said, letting my hand drop to the grass between our legs. "I don't get time with you now, not without Malaki around."

"We really do. You're right." Allison reached her arms above her head, stretching her back cat-like. "Wanna get some food after this?"

"From the best fast-food joint in the middle of absolute nowhere?"

Allison laughed. "I mean… the car's already there, so might as well."

A few minutes passed with unspoken words. I resisted the urge to sit up, because that was the first step to leaving. I knew that somewhere, the sun was setting, but for now I couldn't see it. The sky had been dark all day and it would gradually darken from that point on.

I realized that now, more than ever, I had to bring up the topic I'd been afraid to broach. Our time would be cut short any moment now. My heart raced as I tried to figure out how I'd start. How to say it.

Was that a raindrop already, touching my forehead? I shook it away and spoke up.

"I need to be honest with you, Allison."

She was the one to sit up, to break the spell. Or maybe I had, and that was just her reaction. Either way, Allison peered down at me, still on my back, her eyes questioning

"I'm worried about... you know, Malaki. What he could do." She opened her mouth, but I went on in a hurry. "I don't know, I've just been getting weird vibes from him, and you know how he—"

"Kaia." Her voice was so gentle that it stopped me dead in my tracks. "You've been waiting a long time to say that."

Not the response I expected, by any means. Her expression was understanding, almost pitying, and I couldn't think of anything fitting to say next. I let the moment pass and waited for her to break it.

"Do you think he'll hurt me?" She asked it without a sliver of anger or fear. Just interest.

I stumbled over my answer. "I... he... He just seems pissed off lately. Or something."

Allison rested her hand on my thigh and nodded. "It's okay, Kaia. Me and him are doing really well. He's been talking with me more, wanting to spend time with me, go places around town. We went on a long hike the other day, and it was wonderful." She chuckled. "I guess as long as you feed a man, he's happy, you know? Weird creatures."

"But he... You see it too?" I cocked my head. "You see his temper?"

"I see it, but I also see that he's changed. Or at least, he's trying. Thank you for being concerned, but I also need *you* to trust *me* and stop worrying about it." Kaia rose to her feet laboriously, groaning as her knees popped. "Come on, Kaia. It's starting to rain. I'll explain on the way to the car."

I'd been so invested in her response I didn't notice the rain beginning to pick up. Now that I paid attention, a fat drop splashed against my skin every few seconds. Allison offered a hand and I held it, climbing to my feet. Then our arms drooped to our sides and we started over the grass, toward the road. The interstate fell behind us and more rain fell from the sky. Quicker, harder, heavier, touching my nose and shoulders and cheeks.

"I think that... that getting married kind of woke him up," Allison said, leading the way across the hilltop. "He depends on me now. He's so, like, unable to do things, it's embarrassing. He can't cook, can barely do his own laundry. So, I think he's seeing that he needs me, and he's softened."

I glanced down at the interstate while she elaborated, savoring that view, wondering if we'd ever come back. Wondering if she was telling the truth. —Well, I *could* believe Malaki was a spoiled little brat who didn't know how to do anything, but could he really be growing? Getting better?

"Are you sure, Allison?"

"It's okay, it really is. We had a good talk earlier today. Malaki... he's definitely softened up a bit, in private. I know he still drives like a crazy person and he tries to look cool, but... when it's just us, in our home? He seems... different. Better. Like I said, he needs me." She grinned with something like pride. "And I need you to trust me."

I chewed on her words for a moment. We approached the road and turned right, heading along the overpass, on top of the world. Everything rushed by below us, the busy people racing against time, moments zooming by, thoughts left untouched.

But Allison and I, we basked in the downpour, our shirts clinging to our bodies, water seeping down my neck. At least, with her, I didn't have to rush. I didn't have to race. I could just be. It was the first time in a while I'd felt that way. Not worrying about college or the farm or New Haven. Just her.

"I believe you," I said at last. My voice must've given it away, because I didn't fully mean it.

"Kaia, I promise you. I'm really happy with him." Allison stopped all of a sudden. We were at the center of the overpass now. She gripped both my hands and smiled with her lips, her eyes, her touch. "I'm really happy."

I took a deep breath and threw my arms around her. Both of us were slightly soaked at this point, and the rain grew louder and louder with each passing second. "Then I'm really happy for you, Alley cat."

"Aw, I forgot you used to call me that." She pulled back, blushing, dripping, sparkling. "Let's run, don't ya think?"

I took off past her, and Allison whipped into action. We sprinted across the remainder of the overpass, splashing little puddles, my socks almost as wet as my shoulders. It started to absolutely pour, torrents of rain bashing the sidewalk and our unsuspecting heads. I laughed loudly, spun around in a circle, and nearly tripped in the Dairy Queen parking lot. Allison unlocked her car deftly and slid into the front seat, not caring that she would soak into the fabric. I jumped in the passenger's side, throwing my head around, flinging water all over her and the dashboard.

"You jerk!" she howled with amusement, cowering against the window. "God, I've missed you, Kaia."

"I missed you too." I smirked at her and glanced down at my shirt. "I guess we're getting drive-through, huh?"

"I think you're right. They wouldn't let us inside. Not after this wet t-shirt contest."

"Oh, shut up," I laughed.

Ten minutes later, we were back in the same parking spot,

now with two bags of greasy food. I had a burger on my lap and a thing of fries between my legs, with another meal in the bag to give Nathaniel when I got back to the house. Allison had the same meal as me, with a milkshake instead of the fries. Of course, we ended up sharing both the drink and the fries. It was the exact same meal we'd eaten countless times as highschoolers. I didn't know if she'd purposely copied our old habit or not, but I found it sweet.

Rain battered the windshield, wind ripped at the doors, but inside this car, we were untouchable. Like the world outside didn't even exist. We were alone, together, and at peace. It felt so refreshing, I spent a lot of the time worrying it would end. It had to, of course, but in hindsight, I shouldn't have been that obsessed with it. Should've just enjoyed the moment with her. All of them.

"I remember this one time," Allison began, covering her mouth with a hand, "we sat right here in your old car. That truck from your dad."

"Oh, yeah?" I raised an eyebrow. "And what happened?"

"We just talked about stuff. You know, like how we were gonna leave New Haven, get jobs in California, all that." Allison smiled, though her eyes were melancholy. "And now... look at me. I'll be here forever, probably."

"That's okay, Ally." I offered her the container of fries, but she didn't seem to notice. I went on. "I'm afraid to move, really. I wonder if I could just... study environmental science from here, you know?"

"Is that really what you want, though?"

I turned to look outside my window, away from her for just a moment. Sometimes the gaze of a friend is too much, blocks out the truth. I contemplated her question and found my answer. "I don't know. I don't know what I want. But I *could* be the first one to study that here. Do research in all these forests we've got. Maybe that's crazy. Maybe I'm crazy. I'm just... I'm just scared to leave."

Allison nodded, chewing on the last bite of her sandwich. "Right, I understand."

"What happened to all that courage? What happened to our ninth-grade dreams?" I covered my face with two hands and groaned. "Damn it, Ally, I just don't know anymore. You know?"

She chuckled and nodded. Allison reached out a hand and touched my own. "You wanna know what I think?"

"God, yes." I grinned. "That's all I want."

"Kaia..." She squeezed my hand. The rain smacked harder than ever for a moment, drowning out all other sound. Allison waited for a minute, staring into my eyes, and then it softened. And she spoke. "You're too smart, too ambitious, to stay here. This place limits people. And you're limitless. You're incredible. You need to find somewhere with... with dreamers, with *no* limits."

I felt a tear poking at the corner of my eye and blinked hard, trying to kill it. "It's scary. That interstate's scary."

Allison glanced in that direction, at the exit ramp left forever empty. And a twinkle marked her iris as she started the car engine.

"You won't be fighting anyone to get off here, at least. Nobody ever comes back to visit. And, you know..."

She leaned across the middle console and kissed me on the cheek. It was an act so sudden and unexpected, like a bolt of electricity shooting through my body, from my neck to my toes. I shivered, and not from the soaked, cold shirt still clinging to me.

She winked at me and backed out of the parking spot. "You could be the first, in your own way, like that."

CHAPTER 2
NATHANIEL WOODS

Mom and I were on the back porch, watching the storm roll in. Dad had just left the porch to go close up the barn. So just the two of us, with angry, dark clouds overhead. The whole sky was a blanket of gray storms. Mom pointed into the distance, said there were sheets of rain coming down. I couldn't see them, but I could feel the thunderstorm building. We were alone.

I'd been waiting for a moment like this because I had something I wanted to ask her. Rumors I'd heard. Not about the house's history this time. About its very active present.

"Hey, Mom…" I glanced at her from the corner of my eye, then focused on the distant fields again. "Can I ask you something?"

"Of course, Nate." She smiled. "Do you want a story?"

"No, not exactly. I just… I heard a rumor the other day. At practice."

"Oh?" Her smile flipped and her eyebrows narrowed. "Not about the Dawes, right?"

"No, no. It's about… Allison's boyfriend, actually."

She sighed and put a hand to her forehead. "You heard about that?"

"What?"

"I think we've heard the same thing." She rubbed the edge of the table with a finger, her eyes unfocused. "About the car?"

I gulped. "Yeah. I heard he was going up to the abandoned house. In that red car. Like... a few times."

Mom nodded, raising her eyes slightly to focus on me. "Yes, he... I think Malaki's getting himself into some trouble. I don't know what's gonna end up happening. But it won't be good."

I frowned, thinking only of my sister. "But that means... what if something happens to Allison?"

"I don't wanna think about it." Mom stood from the table, groaning. "Has your sister heard about it?"

"She hasn't mentioned it."

Mom nodded, leaning against the porch railing. Her focus was in the distance again. Dad appeared by the barn, heading this way, with dirt caked on his jeans.

She turned to me with a serious expression. "We don't want your sister to find out, okay? We don't want her to do anything she'll regret."

"You mean go up there?"

Facing away again, she nodded. "Yeah. That's exactly what I mean, Nate. So I'm not saying lie to her, okay? But be smart. Just be smart."

<> <> <>

In the middle of the night, when I opened my eyes, I thought it was the storm that woke me. The rain hammered the roof and wind smacked against the side of our house. It was enough to wake anybody, really, so I laid there quietly for a few minutes, unsure what to listen for or if I could go back to sleep.

The house was completely silent. I didn't want to sit up or

crawl out of bed. The blankets were too warm, the mattress too soft. So instead, I guessed it was around three o'clock, not any later than five. There was no sign of light peeping through the windows, no real way to make out the shapes in my room. Everything had turned to silhouettes. It was creepy, and I didn't wanna look around.

Not that I was afraid of the dark. I was a middle schooler; we didn't get scared of stuff like that. But I closed my eyes anyway, hoping I could drift back into sleep. I fought against my brain for those few minutes, laying in the dark. Listening for anything, shivering anytime the house creaked or groaned. Such an old farmhouse like this, there were guaranteed to be some odd sounds through the night. That thought didn't comfort me though.

A violent thunderclap split the air, somewhere far away. I curled my toes and pulled the blankets up to my chin. Lightning flashed in the sky, sending a pale, blue illumination through the window for just a moment. I swore there was someone in the hallway.

From my bed, I could see my room door, my closet to one side of it, and the MLB poster that hung on the other. When the lightning flashed and then disappeared, I strained my neck to see into the hallway, squinting my eyes, but it was no use. Past my door, there was just a thick mass of darkness, impenetrable.

My heart skipped a beat as I realized something very important. Something that made me grip the blankets and let out a small whimper. I remembered it vividly because I'd made note of it before falling to sleep.

Right before climbing into bed, I changed into a different pair of shorts, so I'd closed the door. It had been like that as I drifted to sleep.

And now it stood wide open.

Yes, Mom might've checked on me. But she usually closed the door after.

"K- Kaia?" I said her name so softly it was more of a whisper, but in the silence of this dead house it carried. My sister was the only other person who slept on the second floor. My parents' bedroom was down below us. "M- Mom?"

Don't jump to conclusions, I chided myself. *Might be nothing.*

When that lightning bolt flashed, there had been a figure, standing awfully close to the wall in the hallway. I was mostly certain of it. Or at least, I had been at the time. Now, though... I didn't want to think about it.

Just go to sleep, you idiot. I closed my eyes hard. Sometimes, if I really, really squeezed them tight, I'd get so tired and fall asleep. But not this time. I couldn't keep them shut. I had to look. I had to watch out for it. If it was anything at all.

Then I heard it. The first knock.

Tap.

It sounded like knuckles on a wall. Outside, in the hallway, near the top of the steps. They came up about halfway between my room and Kaia's. For just a second, I pretended it was the house settling. In the back of my mind, I wondered if I would run to her rescue. If that *thing* moved down toward her room, did I have the strength to chase it down? Save her?

None of that mattered. Because I heard it a second time.

The exact same sound, same volume. But closer to my door.

Tap.

Oh, shit. I held the blanket up to my nose now. Maybe they wouldn't see me. Maybe they would leave. Or it might be Kaia. But I didn't *dare* call out now. I didn't want to hear an answer.

I'd been having nightmares ever since that bike ride, horrible dreams where a burly man chased me with a knife. He wasn't even fully formed, not in any of the scenes. He was just a silhouette man, but I saw his knife in vivid detail, saw it glinting in the moonlight or the lightning or the lamps.

I could almost hear it breathing now. Whatever stood outside my room. Whatever snuck along the wall, grinding its feet into the carpet, holding its hand out. I didn't know if it would stab me or knock again, or if it even mattered. If it would matter at—

Tap.

This time it came from right outside the room. Practically touching the edge of my doorway. It had to be standing at the very edge of the dark mass, had to be watching me from that unbreakable shadow. I cowered and admitted to myself I was afraid of the dark. But maybe it was too late.

Another bolt of lightning in the sky outside. Another clap of thunder in the far distance. As the light carried inside, I watched that door frame. I prayed it would be nothing. My imagination. That was the only explanation left.

Oh my God. There was definitely something there. I saw it leaning around the doorframe. Something tall. Couldn't tell what kind of skin it wore. Could only wait, gasping, and decide.

Should I make a run for it? Could I?

Tap.

It rapped its slimy knuckles against the wall right next to my closet. And I didn't know anything anymore. I felt the most intense fear in my stomach, like hot puke bubbling, my mind entirely blank. Absolutely stuck. I was going to die. I would just accept it. Maybe it wouldn't hurt as bad that way.

One final knock came from the closet itself. I didn't know if it was inside it or not, and I didn't care. It had entered my room, fully. My leg muscles and joints stiffened. I prepared for the worst, a sudden attack.

But twenty seconds passed and I realized it wasn't going to pounce. The creature must have been lurking closer. Crawling across my floor. I could see its slimy mouth and tongue, oozing on the carpet. Each horrific image, creeping nearer to my bed.

I knew that I had to move. I couldn't go down like this.

As silently as possible, I removed the blanket from on top of my legs. I winced as the bedsprings squeaked but still heard nothing. It sounded like I was alone in the room. But I knew better. I knew how this would end if I didn't run.

One… two…

I ground my teeth, fighting against my terror. I would do it. I would leap out of bed and run. The door to the hallway stood open. I just had to avoid the monster on my floor.

Three!

I jumped from my bed, heels smacking the floor, a resounding thump. Without looking over, I dashed to the hallway, gripped the handle behind me, and it crashed shut as I flew through the doorway. I didn't know where I was going or even what to do now, but I sped away.

A scream escaped me as I collided with something.

A sharp pain in my head and then the carpet touched my face. I toppled onto the floor, groaning, throwing my arms out. I felt Kaia to the side of me, where she'd fallen, backward. We lay on the floor, sprawled out. I crawled away from my bedroom, almost falling down the staircase in my haste.

"What the hell, Nate?" she hissed at me, her voice low. Kaia rolled onto her side and peered at me in the dark hallway. I remembered that it was nighttime, that our parents were asleep downstairs. Maybe I'd woken them with my jumping and screaming. I honestly hoped so.

"There's something in my room!" I said, covering my mouth.

Kaia chuckled and started to her feet. "Jesus, kid. That's why you were jumping around and shit?" I started to agree, until she explained further. "You're just afraid of the dark?"

"No, seriously!" I pleaded with her, my knees pressing into the carpet now, the stairs behind me. "Let's go to your room, Kaia, it might—"

"Nathaniel, come on. Get back in bed." She rolled her eyes and offered me a hand to stand up.

"It wasn't me moving around!" I said. "It was coming from my closet, and I saw him sneak through the door—"

"Let's go see, then." She raised an eyebrow but still had that stupid grin on her face.

"Wait, Kaia, no!"

She didn't heed my warning. Kaia moved toward my door, reaching for the handle. I stumbled to my feet, regaining my balance on the wall. She twisted it and stepped inside, flicking the light switch as she went. It blinded us both.

I expected there to be a hulking mass on my bed or something that stepped around the corner with a devilish, lip-licking growl.

But nothing happened. Kaia progressed into the room and did a once-over, opening the closet doors, even stooping to look under my bed. When she faced me again, she shrugged.

"It's like three AM. Come on, man."

"I don't understand…" I came closer to my room, bare feet dragging through the carpet fibers. "I… Kaia…"

She huffed and moved closer. "Fine, Nate. Just sleep on my floor or whatever. I'm tired as hell." Kaia offered me a sympathetic look and stepped past me, heading to her own room.

I hurriedly grabbed a couple blankets and a pillow from my bed, not daring to look around. The room had returned to its eerie silence, with only the thunderstorm and aggressive rain as distractions. I thought I'd see him in the corners, standing with the knife, but I didn't look. Instead, I lowered my head, barreled out the door once again, and shut off the light.

The storm continued as I entered Kaia's room, and actually sounded louder from there. She was already in bed, eyes shut. At least our parents hadn't woken up, I guess. They would've been angrier than her about late night shenanigans. Maybe Mom would've understood, though.

As I came in and started to lay out the blankets, Kaia whispered, "You okay?"

"Yeah..."

I formed a bed out of what I'd brought and curled up in it, facing away from the door. Kaia, above me, turned over on her mattress. Neither of us spoke as the lightning struck again and flashed in our eyes.

"You don't need to be afraid, you know," Kaia said, stifling a yawn. She moved around in bed for a moment, then all fell quiet. "Nothing's gonna hurt us in our own home."

"If you say so..."

I heard it one more time that night, after Kaia had fallen asleep. A faint, subtle knocking. All the way down the hallway, inside my room, I could just barely hear it.

This time, I didn't hide from it and I didn't close my eyes. I stared at the open door, expecting something to appear. Nothing did. The sound died away, as quietly as it'd come.

I was safe in this room with my sister. But for how long?

Something was stirring. Something bad was coming. I only

hoped Kaia would believe me when I told her.

CHAPTER 3
ON THE EDGE OF NEW HAVEN

It was a nasty night for driving. The hills were dripping with water, sending streams down to New Haven, floods building in the low parts of the town. Lightning split the dark sky and cast eerie shadows on every tree, touching every part of the landscape. Allison shivered in the passenger's seat of Malaki's convertible, this time with the roof up.

"Is it safe to be driving out here?" she asked him, her fingers resting on the door handle.

"Sure it is." Malaki gripped the steering wheel with two hands. His eyes kept darting over to her, then ahead of them. There was only one house out here. Only one possible destination. They both knew it.

Allison felt a pang of anxiety every time his gaze crept over toward her. Malaki was acting strange, without a doubt. He looked disheveled as he said he had a surprise for her, and now she realized they were heading to the abandoned house. But that in itself wouldn't terrify her. She didn't believe in ghosts, hauntings, any of that. She did believe in bad motives, and she couldn't make out Malaki's.

The rain battered his car so aggressively it drowned out the engine altogether. The roads were dark, shimmering with a layer of water, turning them into black mirrors. Where the pavement ended and the grass began, it was impossible to tell. The towering trees on either side formed a sort of long, rolling corridor that the car sped down. Up one hill, down it, cresting the next. Getting closer.

Lightning flashed again and painted the abandoned house in its pale, haunting light. Sharp rooftop angles and a cracking exterior. The daunting mass, three stories tall, branching out in either direction. Cold stone and decaying wood, strangling vines. Allison shook her head at the sight of it. Nothing about this felt romantic. It was just creepy. Disturbing.

"Maybe we should come back tomorrow?"

Malaki scoffed. "Of course not. This is perfect."

"I don't mind to wait for your surprise, baby…"

Malaki turned to face her for just a moment and his eyes were glowing. "We have to see it now. It's so exciting, trust me. This is perfect."

Within a few minutes, Malaki pulled into the area next to the house, slabs of concrete covered in high grass. There was a mold-covered fountain on one side of the house, the remains of a garden on the other. Hedges that had gone crazy and weeds strangling whatever once grew there.

He hopped out, staring up at its massive structure with wide eyes. Allison fidgeted with her door handle, climbed out of the car, and stood by its hood. Regular Malaki would've opened the door for her. And wouldn't have brought her here.

She hugged herself tightly and checked that her phone was in her pocket.

"I don't like this, Malaki." What was this, some perverted fantasy from high school? He wanted to "get it on" in the old, abandoned house? She definitely hadn't consented to this. Malaki often crossed the line but never like this.

He reached for her hand. She took it reluctantly, and he started to draw her toward the front door of the house.

I'll be a good wife. Fill this weird fantasy. And he'll make up for this later, she told herself. *Or I'll make him feel terrible, once this is all over. Either way, he owes me one. Or five.*

"It'll be worth it once we're inside, I promise." He grinned. "Just trust me. Just five minutes."

Allison moved with him, approaching the decrepit front door with its twisting brass knocker and paint almost entirely chipped off. Every surface of the house was worn, like its best days had been a century ago, as if nobody had cared for its exterior in almost as long. The porch steps were creaking, threatening to break with each step. When her foot came down, Allison expected it to crumble, to drop her into an endless pit. But the porch held up, and so they were inches away from the door now.

"I don't wanna play this game…" She wanted to say, *I don't believe in ghosts, but the way you're looking at me scares me.*

Malaki reached out and touched the doorknob. As his skin met the cold brass, he smiled even wider, even darker. Then he twisted it and let the door swing open. They were faced with an intense depth of nothing. No eyes could penetrate such empty and dead air. It was like a thick fog, blocking all vision and sound. Until Malaki stepped back and gestured for her to enter.

"Ladies first."

Allison gritted her teeth, told herself it would all be over soon. Just a stupid game. He was testing her. Wanted to mock her for being afraid. Well, she would show him, and then she would scream at him for being such a jerk. She'd make him feel terrible about all this.

But first, she had to take these steps, prove her courage.

"I hate you sometimes," she muttered. Her foot touched the floor inside the house and then her other one followed. Malaki's hands were warm on her back, firm, and she didn't resist.

"You'll like it in here," he whispered. "Just wait til the hallway."

As Allison moved out of his way, Malaki slammed the door shut. They were thrown into intense, impenetrable darkness. She lost all sight and her sense of direction. It was like being trapped under the earth, imprisoned in a grave.

Allison felt Malaki's hands on her back and then other fingers wrapped around her forearm.

CHAPTER 4
KAIA WOODS

Across the road from our house, the forest was a magical place. A few days after the heavy rainstorm, it tingled with life, like it breathed on its own.

I stood at the tree line, marveling. Water droplets clung to leaves from the morning's light showers. They would drip down, touch my forehead as I passed through. Warm rays of sunlight beamed down through the canopy, with bugs dancing around them, spinning in circles. I couldn't help but smile. At the dew on my toes, at the sticks and bramble under my bare feet, at everything.

That forest would never feel quite the same.

Nate ran ahead of me. He veered off path and into some underbrush. I didn't have any shoes, so I stayed on the trail. Let the mud seep between my toes and the earth's energy climb up through my legs. I could hear his laughter up ahead, and sometimes he'd call back to me, the words indecipherable. I loved being out here with him.

Anything to get him away from that Xbox, I told myself. But the truth was — well, honestly, I'd never expected to actually *like* my brother. To enjoy his company. And I did, now. I guess our family was pretty close.

"Will you slow down?" I called ahead, laughing at his excitement.

He didn't answer. The Wolf Cave swam into view ahead of us, the walls perfectly rugged and firm. The shingled roof was covered in water droplets, sunlight, and insects. At the front of the shelter, Nate stood, watching the bubbling creek about ten yards away.

On the way over, we'd crossed the bigger section of that creek, and I'd been nervous for him. The usually calm water, with the help of two thunderstorms, had turned into aggressive rapids. But Nate had tightroped the log without any problems and I'd followed after.

That natural bridge was always my favorite part, standing above the deepest section of water. Looking in either direction, I could see for what felt like miles, all the way to the bend in the creek. The trees on both sides framed it, with fog collecting right above the water. Such a perfect sight. I would miss it after I moved away.

"Look at these little frogs." Nate moved closer to the creek, squatting on the pebbles. It was shallow down here by the Wolf Cave, and perfect for observing. "Just little tadpoles, right by the edge."

I ducked into the Wolf Cave and grabbed a lawn chair. "Cool. How many you think?"

While I set up my chair, I placed the novel I'd brought on the flat surface of the front wall. I had about fifty pages left. This was as good a day as any to finish it.

"Too many to count," he said.

I let him focus on the tadpoles and didn't ask any more questions. Instead, I took a seat, reaching for my book, and propped up my feet where it had been. Taking a deep breath, I sunk into the alternate reality of the pages.

The forest has a way of sparkling around you when you aren't looking. I loved to sink into other worlds, vaguely aware of the beauty surrounding me.

The pages seemed to turn themselves. I devoured the words as they painted vivid images. Sometimes, I'd glance up after a few minutes and experience the forest as if for the first time. All the sensations and emotions and colors rushing back, overwhelming me. I reclined, enjoying it all. Nate was in the distance, out of view, but I heard him calling to the birds and animals. He yelled something about "a deer!" and I chuckled.

What amazed me about the forest was how it moved on its own and breathed. If I sat in a chair like that, right at the heart, it was like one, big organism shifting around me. Everything moved in sync, one cohesive unit. The leaves swayed back and forth, the insects crawled along tree trunks, and squirrels jumped from limb to limb.

That blend of animals and trees and nature mesmerized me. I eventually closed the book, placed it on the flat spot again, and let the earth waves wash over me.

Mom could always describe the forest better than me. She told me how she'd spent days in it before, just sitting. Sometimes hiking. (Although she'd admitted there was definitely weed involved at times.) She told me how her and some of those other hippies would say nothing for entire chunks of time, and then one would break the silence, and they'd laugh and speculate.

I wanted friends like that. I wanted that experience. But in New Haven, it was just me and Nate who appreciated the woods like this.

"Hey, Kaia." Nate appeared from deeper in the trees,

holding a huge leaf in one hand. It was as big as his head. "Can we go explore?"

"Exploring, huh?" I smiled and pretended to think hard. "You still know how? Been a while."

"Yeah, duh." He rolled his eyes and placed the leaf gently on his head. Such a quirky kid.

"You're funny." I stood from the chair and emerged from the shelter, moving over next to him. Together, we faced the untamed, unknown section. "Okay. Choose a direction and number."

"Umm... left." Nate paused. "And maybe five."

"You know 'maybe five' isn't a number."

We plunged into the trees to our left, fighting through bushes.

Nate was holding the big leaf in between two fingers now, rolling it back and forth. "You know what I mean, stupid."

I laughed out loud, ruffling his hair. Nate shied away and blushed.

We carried on like that. The two of us strolling like tourists, like window-shoppers, pointing out cool trees or huge bugs or distant animals. Wandering into thorn bushes, dancing around bristle patches, we headed straight for five minutes (checked on my phone). Then, at the base of a hearty, thick tree, we took a moment to look around.

"Alright. You pick now." With hands on his hips, Nate eyed me expectantly.

I turned in every direction, observing. I could hear the gentle gurgle of the creek over there, probably a deep spot. And over there, opposite, there was some kind of clearing. Or at least a place with easier ground. I could see the grass, just barely, and the way light bends at the tree line. I gestured at it.

"That way. *Ten* minutes. Should put us in that clearing or whatever it is."

Nate nodded. "Sounds good."

So, we took off again, Nate leading the way. The rough ground from earlier gave way to more soil, less roots. Thankfully, too, since the soles of my bare feet were starting to hurt. There were birds to our right, singing loudly in their tree, and what sounded like a woodpecker to the left. Nate still gripped his huge leaf. We approached the edge of the trees.

It wasn't a big clearing, just a patch of tall grass. But as we stepped out of the shade, I caught a whiff of something sweet and floral. Like springtime. I moved ahead, into the high weeds, and found a patch of flowers. Blue, with white centers, pink dotting the edges. The light struck them in a certain way, and the morning rain still sprinkled their petals. I knelt by them and took a picture with my phone. Then I stood back to appreciate it.

Nate ran up beside me and watched them, swaying in the breeze with blades of grass. We stood like that for a few minutes, just observing. I touched the petals of one and shuddered at its smoothness and beauty. They reminded me of Allison, in a way.

I would love to bring her out here. I hadn't seen her in a few days, but the memory flooded back. Sitting on the hillside. Running through the rain. Sharing a meal. Sharing a moment.

"Are you leaving soon?" Nate asked.

The question caught me off guard. I turned to look at him. "What?"

He chewed on his lip. "For... college?"

"Oh." I turned back to the flowers, sighing. "Yeah. In a couple months. I still have to decide where."

"And you're gonna study nature?"

My heart swelled. I gently nodded and knelt down to caress

the flowers again. "Yeah, I will."

"That's cool." Nate hesitated. I felt him shifting from side to side, struggling with something he wanted to say. I didn't push him. After a minute, he continued. "I want you... to teach me. When you come back and visit. Like, whatever cool stuff you learn."

I resisted the temptation to "aww" and tell him how sweet that was, how adorable. Instead, I gently plucked one of the flowers, near the base, and handed it to him. Nate eyed me suspiciously, holding it the same way he would a Barbie doll.

"Take it," I insisted, rising to my feet. "Give it to Mom. She'd love that."

He obliged and held it next to his giant leaf.

"And yeah, I'll tell you all sorts of stuff when I come back." I reached out and tousled his hair again, though he hated it and pulled away. "You won't even miss me that much, you know."

He shrugged, not taking the bait. But as we moved away from the clearing and back into the trees, I thought he mumbled, "I might."

"Can we go back to the Wolf Cave?" he asked me, not turning around. "I'll keep the flower there 'til we leave."

"Good idea," I said, high-stepping over an angry-looking bush. "I'm gonna finish my book before we explore more. It'll take, like, twenty minutes."

As we maneuvered back through the forest, retracing our steps, Nate kept glancing over at me, like he wanted to say something. I waited patiently.

"Hey, Kaia, do you... do you believe in ghosts?"

I raised my eyebrows. "I think so. Why?"

"I was just thinking about it after... what happened the other night."

"Oh, right." I'd honestly forgotten about his nighttime episode. I'd chalked the whole thing up to a nightmare or something. Maybe a story some kid told him at practice. "You think you saw a ghost?"

"No, not really." He shrugged, staring into the distance as we pushed through a heavy patch of underbrush. "I'm not sure what it was."

"Well, I think they're real, yeah. But if you ever get scared, you can come in my room. Maybe it's safer."

"It feels safer."

"That's really all that matters. If it feels safer to you, then you won't be as scared."

He nodded and seemed to think about what I'd said, as we pushed toward home base.

We didn't have any problems finding our way back. Some afternoons when we explored, the two of us would have to get to the creek and trek along that, but today there weren't any issues. The Wolf Cave peered at us through the tree trunks. Nate turned to me.

"You think it'll ever fall down?"

I shrugged. "Not for a few years, I think. Unless we get a tornado or something."

He accepted this answer and hurried ahead. I watched as he vanished through the thicket and ducked inside the structure.

Nathaniel placed the flower on the chair I'd been using. I glanced around for my book, not sure exactly where I'd placed it. Not on the arm of the chair and not on the flat surface of the front wall. I started to search on the ground, thinking it might've fallen, crouching down to inspect under the chair. There was no sign of it.

"Hey, Nate?" I called for him without looking up. "Did you

grab my book?"

"What? Me?"

I straightened up, turning all around, scratching my head. "Yeah... You seen it?"

"No." He was distracted by the tadpoles in the creek again.

"Alright, then." I racked my brains for anywhere else it might've fallen or I might've put it. The book didn't turn up over the next few minutes, despite my best efforts. I wasn't even that worried about losing it, 'cause I could always buy the e-book and finish what I had left to read. More than anything, I just felt confused. It didn't make sense for a book to disappear like that.

Maybe Nathaniel moved it somewhere.

As I started to walk over to his spot by the creek, my phone buzzed against my hip. I grabbed it and saw my dad's caller ID. Pressing the button, I raised it to my ear and said, "Dad?"

"Where are you?"

I frowned. "Um... in the forest. With Nate."

Nate turned around and raised his eyebrows.

"Get back here as quick as you can." My dad's voice was unusually rough, with a hint of some other emotion I couldn't quite name.

"Is something wrong?" I gestured for Nate to come over from the creek. He stood up, mouthed a question to me, but I didn't have time to respond before Dad continued.

"Sheriff Wheeler's here and he wants to... to ask you some questions." I recognized the emotion now. He was worried, or more aptly he was terrified. "Just get back here and we'll get it sorted out."

"Okay, Dad. Do you know what's wrong, though?"

There was static for a moment. "Just come home." And then he hung up.

I reached for the flower and handed it to Nate as I stored the phone in my pocket. Our eyes met and his begged for answers. I fidgeted on the spot, uncertain what next step to take. It would take us ten or fifteen minutes to get back to the house, so we really needed to get going. But my legs wouldn't move right away. I could only speculate. Two unanswerable questions. Where was my book and what did the sheriff want? At least one of those would be a closed case soon enough.

"What's going on?" Nate finally asked.

"We need to go back to the house," I said, glancing at him. He watched me, wide-eyed and curious, but when I continued, his face grew pale. "I don't know what's wrong, but…"

"What, Kaia?"

I gulped. "Dad said the sheriff wants to talk with me."

Nathaniel placed the flower on my lawn chair. He gathered his shoes, acting quickly. I didn't pay attention. I was standing at the edge of the creek, staring down at the bubbling water, thinking hard for an explanation. All thoughts of the missing book were gone. I just wanted to know *why* the sheriff needed me.

My first thought was childish; a speeding ticket, maybe. But then I realized there was only one reason why the sheriff would come for *me*. It had to be about Allison.

Had something happened to her? Did Malaki do it?

Was she okay?

Nate hurried to my side, leaving behind the flower. It remained in the Wolf Cave, where it would rot, the blue and pink turning to gray and death.

"I'm sure it's okay," Nate said, patting me awkwardly on the back of my shoulder. He attempted a consoling smile and led the way down our narrow trail. Toward home and whatever waited there.

"I hope so." My voice sounded foreign. My heart felt ready to explode. "But I'm not sure."

The forest had lost much of its appeal. We trekked back, and the greenery was tinted with gray and darkness. Nate didn't speak. In fact, he barely looked at me.

If something had happened to Allison, I wouldn't be okay. I already felt my breaths, coming quick and shallow, and my legs shaking.

I needed her to be okay.

CHAPTER 5
BENJAMIN "CLIFF" WOODS

When the white patrol car rattled up our driveway, I was standing in the barn. The big sliding doors were wide open, so I saw him coming, kicking up dust. The car seemed to fly down our driveway. I barely had time to set down my tools and march outside.

Leaving the dirty barn floor with hay strewn all over the place, I turned my back on the tractor — I'd been fixing it all day, laboring in the heat. I met him outside, on the gravel. The sheriff pulled his car right up to the barn's edge and hopped out. I waited there, leaning against the exterior wall, my arms folded.

"What can I do for you, Sheriff?"

Ten minutes and one phone call to Kaia later, we were in that same position. The sheriff kept looking past me, at the house, and seemed eager to head over there. I heard Naomi's footsteps crunching toward us, likely from the back porch. Sheriff Wheeler glared at her, then quickly turned his gaze to me.

"What's taking 'em so long?"

"They're out in the woods, Sheriff," I huffed. "We weren't exactly expecting visitors."

"Right." He kicked at the gravel and touched the brim of his star-emblazoned hat. "How do ya do, Naomi?"

"Better ten minutes ago." She stopped beside me and crossed her arms.

I consciously unfolded mine and stuffed both hands in my jean pockets. "We can wait on the deck for the kids. That's the best place for a talk like this."

"What's this about, anyway?" Naomi asked, her tone biting.

"I'll tell ya when the kids get here." He planted both elbows on the top of his patrol car, smirking. He seemed to enjoy holding this secret knowledge over our heads.

"Is it about the Dawes?" Naomi continued to prod.

He laughed, darkly. "No, ma'am. I've got all the info I need on them." He cleared his throat and added, absent-mindedly, "Did you know old Malaki had a run-in with the Smith boy last week? See, I didn't know that 'til recently. Odd timing, I do say."

"It's not exactly *news* that Malaki's an asshole," Naomi snapped. "He's also been meddling up at that house."

"No, we didn't know that," I said. I tried to shoot her a look, but she avoided my gaze.

Had there always been this much animosity between her and the sheriff? After what she'd told me about him, maybe so. My wife was the kindest, calmest person in the world, except when it came to one man.

Then again, he was here to interrogate our daughter. Maybe I should've been more furious myself. I just felt confused and tired. Ready for some answers and to send this man away from our home.

Nobody spoke for a few minutes, so I stared at the distant tree line across the road. I thought I saw movement there, like the kids returning. I took this opportunity to move our showdown from the driveway to the back porch. Naomi went ahead to set up the chairs and probably a glass of lemonade. I waited with the sheriff for just a moment. When I was certain there were two figures moving across the distant field, I brought him around back as well.

Sheriff Wheeler, hat firmly on his head, strolled alongside me. He glanced over at my barn, at the chickens who were strutting around their outside, fenced-in area, and then his watchful gaze turned to our home again. I didn't like the way he stared at it, like he was searching for weak spots or something.

"Beautiful day, isn't it?" I offered, as we turned into the back yard.

"Not when you've seen what I have," the sheriff muttered. He let out a deep breath and shook his head. "Awful things, Cliff…"

"But you still aren't gonna tell us?"

"All in good time."

He followed me up the three wooden steps and onto the back porch. The sheriff looked around, reached inside a pocket, and pulled out a toothpick. He started chewing on it as he took a seat at the table.

Naomi and I took our seats carefully. We were on one side of the table, with the sheriff next to me. Across from us, there were three seats. Enough for a buffer seat between the sheriff and where the kids would sit. I hoped Nate would let his sister get closest to Naomi.

As we waited in awkward, tense silence, Naomi caught my eye every few minutes, her expression wary. I reached for her hand, but she pulled away. He'd been here for fifteen minutes, and still neither of us knew why the man had come. But we both understood the severity of the situation. Or at least, we thought we did.

"You know..." The sheriff fidgeted with the calluses on his palms as we waited for the kids to appear. "You two don't necessarily need to be—"

"Sheriff, all due respect, we aren't leaving." I shook my head.

Naomi snorted when I said the "all due respect" part. She sat frighteningly still, like a statue, her livid gaze drifting from the big oak tree to the sheriff.

He tried to avoid looking at her as we waited. His eyes were usually trailing over me or the view from our porch, but never Naomi. She must've frightened him. He should've known better than to come for our kids.

"It's a shame, really, that I had to come out here." The sheriff clicked his tongue, still chomping away on that toothpick. "But a man's gotta do his job."

"Right, you keep hinting at stuff, but are you ever gonna tell us?" Naomi asked testily. "Or are you just here to stir up trouble?"

The sheriff narrowed his eyes and toyed with the badge on his chest. I couldn't tell if this movement was supposed to be threatening or absent-minded. "I'll tell you all when the girl gets here."

"You know her name is Kaia," Naomi corrected him, "and why wait? I wanna know what you're accusing her of before she walks into this—"

"We're just concerned," I butted in, throwing a look at her. My wife stared back with such vitriol that I couldn't hold her gaze for long. "Sheriff, can't you tell us anything?"

"I ain't here about the Dawes," he said, speaking slow, like he was carefully choosing what to reveal. "But as far as Smith goes, I've got my suspicions. That family lives a few blocks from where the fire happened. And I've seen firebugs. That boy shows all the signs."

"That's ridiculous," Naomi responded with a forced laugh. "Smith? He's harmless."

Sheriff Wheeler raised his eyebrows. "Oh, really? Not how Malaki described him."

Naomi folded her arms. "I wouldn't trust a single word coming out of that boy's disease-infested mouth."

I sighed. "Naomi—"

"No. You've heard what Kaia's said about him. He's not trustworthy. If anything, *he's* the one you should suspect."

Sheriff Wheeler frowned. "Don't tell me how to do my job, miss."

The kids would arrive any minute. I shared a look with Naomi, who took a deep breath and tried to ignore the sheriff for the next few minutes. Her expression said, "I'm fine. Stop worrying about me," but I found that task impossible.

The two of them finally appeared by the corner of the house. Both faces were uncertain, peering around, as if they thought they were in trouble. Kaia's eyes locked onto her mom, and I thought I saw another emotion there. Fear.

The sheriff smirked, his eyes wild. "Glad you kids finally made it back," he called out. "Kaia, would you mind takin' a seat?"

As Nathaniel and Kaia approached the back porch, the air thickened with tension. Even the gentle breeze sweeping across our fields couldn't ease it. The soybeans shivered from its touch, and I looked out there, longingly. That was a world I understood better. That was peaceful and simple. This... this was dangerous.

"I got some questions for you." The sheriff gestured to one of the empty chairs.

I gritted my teeth. It felt like he was purposefully doing

things to set off Naomi now, like barging in before she could speak, trying to steer the conversation. I think he *wanted* her to lose control and chase him away from the property, so he could come back later with a reason to investigate us. Maybe I was just speculating, but it wasn't far-fetched.

Either way, Naomi's knuckles were growing pale as she gripped her knees harder than ever. I extended my hand, again. This time, she held it. Or rather, she used it like a stress ball.

Kaia took a seat next to Naomi, leaving two between herself and the sheriff. Nathaniel stood awkwardly, hand on the back of his neck.

"Nate," I said, "you can—"

"Sit down, son." The sheriff didn't even look at me as he commanded my son. "You should hear this too."

As Nathaniel pulled out the empty chair next to his sister and found a home in it, Naomi spoke up. "Will you tell us *now*, or are you hoping to stay for dinner?" She gave him the iciest smile. "I'll go ahead and answer: no."

Sheriff Wheeler muttered something under his breath and whipped out a notepad from one of his jacket pockets. It had tiny, indecipherable writing lining the pages, but he inspected it carefully before going on. He also spat out the toothpick. It landed on the table.

"I'm here because you" —he pointed to Kaia, and his voice became business-like— "are a well-known acquaintance of Allison Banks. Have you, eh… seen her recently or heard from her?"

Kaia shook her head, biting her lip. "Not in almost a week. We rarely text."

The sheriff chewed on his pen and then scribbled something on the notepad. "Well, you see…" A pause for dramatic effect, and a snarky nod at Naomi. "What happened is simple. Nobody has seen either Malaki or Allison in over three days. They ain't been seen around town, but they never mentioned leaving. They ain't at home. It's like they — to be frank — just vanished."

"But what's that got to do with me?" Kaia was rigid, like her mother, and glanced in my direction for support. "I haven't talked to her in a week." Her lips were twitching. This was her best friend, after all.

"As you say, yes…" Sheriff Wheeler tapped his pen on the table, an even more annoying habit. "Our investigation will proceed, of course, but if there's any… pertinent information you could share, it might help speed things along."

Kaia didn't answer right away. When nobody spoke, she finally asked, "So… what are you asking?"

Naomi smirked. I could tell she and Kaia would be quite a force to reckon with if he wanted to interrogate much further. The two of them could withhold anything they chose, and more importantly they would dance around the sheriff all day long with their wit and snark. It wasn't a fair match, by any means.

"When was the last time you *saw* Allison Banks?" The sheriff raised his notepad like a loaded gun and prepared to jot down her answer.

"About a week ago, like I said." She crossed her arms. "A couple days before the big thunderstorm."

Is that a lie? I stared at the table and thought hard. She'd gone to see Allison sometime recently, but it didn't feel like a week had passed. No, I was fairly sure it was the night *of* the thunderstorm, which meant four or five days ago. Maybe not a lie, then, but stretching the truth.

"And where did you go?"

Kaia scoffed. "I don't think it's relevant, do you?"

The sheriff raised his eyebrows. "I find it *very* relevant, yes.

Where'd you go?"

"We went to that DQ by the interstate and got food."

The questions continued for another ten minutes. It was like a game of tennis, the two of them swinging back and forth. Sheriff Wheeler would press forward and then step back and then press again. Kaia kept her composure the entire time, giving away as little information as possible, never faltering in her story. I was impressed, quite frankly, because the whole thing gave me a searing headache. Naomi held her hand under the table, and the two of them found strength in resistance.

"Are you finished now?" Naomi interrupted after the sheriff had retraced his steps for a third time. "You're not even asking new questions."

The sheriff huffed and glanced at Nathaniel for a second. I wondered about that.

"I do have one more question," Sheriff Wheeler went on. He eyed us each in turn as he spoke. "And some advice. Be careful who you're alone with, who you trust. You've all heard of the new family in town, the Dawes? Yes, well, we have reason to believe they're involved in this. The location of their home plus Malaki's statement... it's something to go on. That's all I can say, for now."

He scribbled something on that dumb pad again. "Nate, you're, uh... you play baseball. Have you, by chance, had much facetime with the Dawes kid? Or talked outside of—?"

"You're not here to interrogate *both* my children, Sheriff." Naomi stood from the table, glaring down at him. "Go inside, Nate."

Nathaniel didn't budge. I felt this was a good time for me to step into the conversation, so I also pushed my chair back and stood.

I let go of Naomi's hand and faced the sheriff. "I think we're done here. Can I speak to you in private, Sheriff?"

I tried to sound firm, but my eyes were pleading with him to let it go. I knew that if he pressed any further with the Dawes questions, Naomi might say something she'd regret. Well, also, I worried she'd expect me to support her. And I still hadn't made my mind up about that family.

"Yes, we're done here." Sheriff Wheeler backed away from the table, collecting his notepad. His cruiser waited just around the corner. "I'm heading to the Dawes house now. Naomi, you can send your *friend* a message and tell her to look out for me."

He tipped his hat to us, as Naomi cursed under her breath. I walked with him for a minute, off the back porch and around to the barn. The sheriff was humming to himself, a tune that sounded familiar, as we crunched our way up the driveway.

"What'd you want to say, Cliff?" He turned to face me, only feet away from his police cruiser. "Don't try to talk me outta this. I'm investigating the Dawes. Nothing you can do about it."

"No, I know. I see that." I took a deep breath and scratched my chin. I had to word this exactly right. "Look, Sheriff, you and I, we've known each other a long time, right?"

He nodded, skeptically. "Yessir, Cliff. That's why—"

"So you know Naomi, she can get a bit heated. But she means well. She's just protecting our kids, you see?"

"Where's this going, Cliff?"

Was I betraying my wife by doing this? Or was I saving our family? It's hard to say when the lines are so blurred.

"Listen, if you... if you leave my family alone, my girls... I'll keep an eye out for you. On Smith. I see him whenever I pick Nate up. And I'll tell you if Naomi hears anything about the mom. Right? I can do that for you. If you leave us alone."

The sheriff chewed on his lip, thinking this over. His eyes scanned my face, and I tried to stand as straight as possible. Chest out, features set in stone.

He smiled, and it gave me chills.

"Yes, Cliff. I think that'll work just fine." He reached out and I reluctantly shook his hand. "I'm glad you're coming around. I knew you weren't an idiot."

"Seriously, though. Malaki's been up at that house. So it might be worth checking out, Sheriff. At least to see if his car's up there."

"Maybe so. Won't be today. Maybe... in a day or two, I'll get around to it."

He nodded thoughtfully and climbed into his car after that. He gave me a thumbs-up through the windshield. I lowered my head and trekked back to the house. I felt like I'd betrayed my family. But I'd done it to save them, right?

If someone was going to feel the sheriff's wrath, I didn't want it to be my family. Sure, I'd try to protect the Dawes if they were proven innocent. But I wasn't going to throw my home, my life, my family in front of a bullet for them. I wasn't going to risk everything for some strangers.

I marched to the back porch, where Kaia and Naomi were still sitting. They looked at me expectantly as I took a seat. There were bugs flying everywhere now, mosquitoes trying to land on my arm. I swatted them away and straightened up.

"Just had to cool things down," I lied.

Right around when the cruiser pulled out onto the main road, Kaia addressed me and Naomi.

"I lied to him," she said, now slouched and hands shaking. "I did get a text from Allison. Two days ago. A couple days after I saw her."

"Two days ago?" I gaped at Naomi, who didn't appear quite as surprised. "You got a text that recently? That's after she went missing, right…"

"Just wait." Kaia pulled out her phone and tapped on the screen. She took a deep breath and then read off the text message to us.

Naomi and I were both stunned into silence after that. She held up her phone screen to prove it was the truth, the little speech bubbles turning my blood cold.

you were right.

i really messed up

i'm so sorry for everything

CHAPTER 6
NAOMI WOODS

It was the kind of day where the empty bleacher seats turned into stovetops and you had to be careful where you placed your hand. Kaia and I were in the top row of the left bleachers. The baseball game was in the second inning, but nobody had scored yet, and Nate hadn't been up to bat. So, in the meantime, Kaia and I were inspecting the crowd around us.

"When's Dad getting here?" Kaia asked me. There was an empty spot to her left, reserved for Cliff. Good thing, too, because the rows were quickly filling with people.

I glanced at my phone, but no notifications. "Don't know. He had to run into town for something."

"Something about the Dawes?"

I looked at her with a sad smile. "I appreciate how concerned you've been, honey, but you don't need to worry about this. Me and your dad will handle it."

Kaia didn't respond. She tapped her foot on the metal surface under us, shoveled popcorn into her mouth, and watched as the last batter before Nathaniel came to the plate. There was only one out, so he'd definitely get to bat this inning.

"I'm worried about Allison," Kaia said, lowering her eyes.

"I texted her, but she didn't answer. I just... I wanna do something to help."

"I understand, honey." I placed a hand on her knee. "They're both missing, though, her and Malaki. So it's really up to the police."

"The same police on a witch-hunt for the Dawes?" Kaia huffed and stared straight ahead. The batter had just collected his second strike and a mixture of cheers and groans rose from the crowd. Those other moms could be *so* loud. "What if he's... What if Malaki has her locked up somewhere? Or worse? That idiot could've drove them both off a cliff."

"I know you're worried, baby. I just don't know if there's anything we can do right now."

She didn't answer me and she stopped eating the popcorn. Our eyes turned to the baseball game, but I felt a tension radiating from her. I'd been like that once. Desperate to do something, to make an impact, always searching for answers. Things changed, though. I learned that, sometimes, you had to sit still and be quiet. Even if it hurt.

The batter struck out, swinging then slumped back to the dugout. Nathaniel strolled over from where he'd been warming up and stood by home plate. There was nobody on base, two outs, and it looked like the second inning would end in a 0-0 tie. Kaia and I both watched as he gripped the bat, resting it on his shoulder.

"Not a great situation for him," I mumbled. Kaia didn't comment. Maybe she was angry with me.

The first two pitches flew by without a swing. One strike, one ball. Nathaniel shifted in place, leaning forward slightly.

"He's swinging this time," Kaia muttered, almost to herself. "I can tell."

"Oh, yeah?"

The pitcher wound up and let one go, right as Nathaniel picked up his front foot. With a loud crack, the ball and bat collided, and then he took off running.

"Told you!" Kaia whooped.

Nothing like a baseball game to raise her spirits.

All around us, the crowd yelled. The ball flew over second base and collapsed to the grass, where it rolled another twenty feet. Nathaniel rounded first base just as an outfielder reached the ball, and it was obvious neither of them would back down. My son's cleats kicked up dust behind him, now halfway to second. The outfielder threw to second, right as Nathaniel closed in. He dove for the bag, hand outstretched. The umpire called him safe, and I let out an involuntary "Whoo!"

It's not like me to cheer loudly at ball games, but I couldn't help it at times. My son was too good.

Kaia chuckled beside me. "Jesus, he's fast."

I nodded, a swell of pride. "He's a natural out there."

"Wait 'til next year," Kaia reminded me. She handed me the popcorn and leaned back, stretching her arms and shoulders. "He'll be one of the older kids on the team. Nate said he *wants* to hit a homer, but I don't think Dad practiced with him."

I made a mental note to ask Nathaniel if he wanted to practice with me instead. Cliff had been so busy and would only get busier as harvest season approached. I was imagining the two of us in the front yard. Nathaniel would hit baseballs deep into the bean field and I'd cheer every time.

The next batter struck out. Nathaniel jogged back to the dugout from second base, and then returned to that same base, now on defense.

"You think he'll play second base next year still?" I asked her.

"Maybe…" Kaia screwed up her face in thought. "Well, actually, that left outfielder is gonna move up, so …"

Kaia started to tell me about the older kids on the team who would move up to high school ball next year. She knew the age and skills of everyone on the team. She'd been to almost every game so far, and I appreciated the insight (especially about Nathaniel's potential on next year's team), but my mind wandered elsewhere at that moment.

It struck me that I hadn't seen Anne Dawes anywhere in the bleachers. I hadn't seen Smith around the dugout, either. He didn't ever get to play, but he usually showed up somewhere, at least in warmups. I glanced at the other set of bleachers, mostly fans of the away team, but she wasn't there either. Anne Dawes would stick out like a sore thumb in this crowd, even without her two children. No, I felt confident she wasn't here. And that unnerved me.

"Was Smith at practice this week?" I turned to Kaia, who had picked up Nathaniel both times.

Kaia chewed on her answer for a moment. "Yeah, pretty sure. Him and Nate were talking one day when I pulled up."

"I don't see him here," I pointed out. "Or his mom."

Kaia did a similar once-over of the crowd and agreed with me that no Dawes were present. But her gaze and attention returned to the baseball diamond right after. I couldn't focus on it. My mind had wandered to the Dawes house, potential reasons why they wouldn't show up. Sure, maybe Smith had gotten sick or been injured or quite frankly didn't want to come when he never got to play. But it didn't feel right. Especially not with Cliff running off to meet Jeremy.

He'd told me as we'd parted ways in the parking lot that Jeremy needed to meet him. Something urgent, it sounded like.

But with no specifics, I came to save him a seat. Now waiting for him to return, I replayed our conversations from that week.

Ever since Cliff had gone to visit the Dawes house, he'd been reluctant to talk about them. I couldn't figure out why, but it made me suspicious. And now Jeremy needed him? And the Dawes hadn't shown up? It all hinted at bad, bad news.

Maybe Kaia's right, I thought to myself. *Maybe we need to do something after all.*

Kaia wanted to save her friend if possible. And I wanted to defend this family of strangers, a mom I'd only spoken to at church. While Kaia didn't have any clear steps ahead of her, I did. I knew what I had to do, or, more specifically, who I needed to confront. Maybe it was time to stop running from it.

The third inning went by without anything eventful. Nathaniel made a nice throw to first, catching someone out, but his team didn't score when they went up to bat. The top of the fourth was the same way. An opposing team's runner actually got to second, but he didn't score, so going into the bottom of the fourth it was still 0-0.

Kaia and I were baking in the heat, roasting in the sun, just to watch a stalemate. The popcorn was gone, too. And Cliff still hadn't shown up. Not the most gripping of performances, by any means, so my mind continued to wander.

"Kaia, have you ever gone up to the abandoned house?"

She looked at me, startled. "Me? No, course not."

I thought about what I wanted to say while our team's first batter struck out. The defensive slugfest continued.

"I have," I said at last.

Her eyes locked onto me. Kaia knew I never talked about that place, especially not with her and Nathaniel. But something about the atmosphere that day made me braver, or at least more open. I had a feeling that Cliff would return with bad news. I knew that it was time to take drastic steps for the Dawes. Things were changing. It was time to stop hiding.

"You have? When?"

"About a year after I moved here." I offered a weak smile as the story progressed. "I don't think I can ever go back. It was a mistake, and it's hard to explain why I did it, but I was lucky to… to get out. That place isn't right, I'm telling you. It's not just creepy, either. It's actually… dangerous."

Kaia raised her eyebrows. "But it's abandoned, isn't it?"

"Hard to say." I paused. "No, I wouldn't say it's… totally empty. So I'm gonna try to convince the sheriff to check it out. To make sure."

The crowd cheered as someone finally hit a ball, though they only got to first base. I waited for the noise to die down. Nathaniel would be up again soon. I needed to explain, while I still had her attention, but it was such a hard thing to relive.

If Allison didn't turn up, Kaia would turn to the one place left. The mystery hanging over her, like it hung over anyone who grew up in New Haven. It was the one shadow which might hold answers, a daring choice for a desperate friend. There were always rumors about that house. Malaki's red convertible driving up there. And he'd been in town, bragging. Even Nate had heard about it.

I wondered if he'd told his sister. Or if Kaia might've heard the rumors on her own. And if she had…

I had been just like her when I came to its lifeless doors. I hoped I could warn her, before it was too late. Before she made the same mistake I had.

"It's like something lives in there," I said, not meeting her eyes. Maybe I should've. "Something… evil. It's been there all along. It's grown. And I'm starting to think it's not stuck inside anymore."

CHAPTER 7
CLIFF WOODS

We'd just pulled up to the gravel lot outside the baseball field when Jeremy called me. I almost didn't answer. I was going to my son's game, after all.

As Naomi and Kaia climbed out of the truck, I checked my phone.

"Sorry, it's Jeremy," I said to Naomi, holding it up.

She stood there, hands on her hips, scowling. "Go on," she said to Kaia. "Get us a good seat, will you?"

Kaia headed off for the baseball field. The bleachers were already filling in, only ten minutes 'til first pitch. We'd dropped Nathaniel off half an hour ago, so he could stretch and warm up with the team. With ten minutes until the game, the sun was already murderously hot, and if my own son wasn't playing there was no chance in hell I'd sit through it. But for Nathaniel, I would do that and more.

"Hey, Jeremy." I held the phone to my ear and mouthed "I'm sorry" to my wife.

She shrugged and leaned both elbows against my truck bed.

Jeremy's words poured through the speaker all at once. "Cliff thankgod listen. Yougotta meetme. Where're you?"

I frowned. His voice sounded panicked. "The ball field. Nate's got a game, Jeremy, so you'll have to wait—"

"No, no, listen. I'm in town. It won't take long." He paused, breathing heavily. "Head toward Main, 'kay? I'll meet you. Won't take long."

"Jeremy—"

"*Cliff*. It's big."

And then he hung up.

Naomi tapped a finger to her wrist. "It's almost time." Her expression shifted. "What'd Jeremy want?"

"He said..." I scratched at my chin and shook my head. "He wants to meet. I'm gonna run over to Main Street, okay? It won't take long."

Naomi sighed. "Fine, but it better not. You know Nate wants you here."

"I know, I know." I moved around the truck bed to give her a kiss. "I'll be so quick you won't even notice I'm gone."

She rolled her eyes but smiled. "Okay, go on." She shooed me away with a hand. "I'm not saving any popcorn for you, though."

I turned my back on her and jogged off in the direction of Main Street. There were more people climbing out of their cars now. The gravel parking lot had a thin cloud of dust hanging over it. I charged through, making a straight line for the nearest alley. It only took about five minutes before my armpits were damp, my lungs heaving, and I slowed to a brisk walk.

When I reached the alleyway, I found Jeremy jogging through it from the other side. He turned off Main Street and met my gaze. His hair was all over the place, sweat dripping from his nose, and his face had turned bright red, like it always did when he worked hard. But more noticeable than anything, his eyes were wide, staring through me.

"Cliff. Thank God."

He leaned against the brick wall beside us and breathed heavily for a moment. I stood there, waiting for him to catch his breath and give me some answers. Beyond him, Main Street seemed deathly quiet. There were very few cars bumbling past, and no pedestrians. Maybe everybody had gone to the baseball game. There'd been a sizable crowd there when I left, but it still felt strange. Something about New Haven wasn't quite right this afternoon.

"So, what's going on?" I asked him, crossing my arms.

"Cliff... oh, man, this is hard to say..."

I groaned in frustration. "Jeremy, come on." There were cheers rising from the crowd behind us now, all the voices muffled together. The distant sound of a baseball hit by a bat. "I've gotta get to my kid's game. I need you to explain, 'kay?"

"I'm sorry, I know." Jeremy shook his head. He refused to meet my gaze now. His own drifted past me, toward the baseball field. "Looks like the whole town's over there... that's for the best, I think."

"Yeah, okay."

"I'm sorry to pull you away from it, Cliff. But I had to tell you in person. It's... about Malaki."

"Oh?" I certainly hadn't expected that.

Jeremy's face turned pale and ashen, like he'd seen a ghost. He nodded, slowly. "You know he'd been going up to the house? He was in town, bragging about it. I heard him myself."

"Yeah. Naomi mentioned it."

"Well..." He took a deep breath. "He turned up at the police station.

"He did? And... Allison?"

Jeremy shook his head, gravely.

"Malaki came back, really freaked out, lookin' like death. Drove his car up, ran inside, and told them... Well, he told everyone he'd been up at that house, with Allison, and he says the Dawes boy was up there, doing some kinda ritual. Kept them both up there, until he managed to escape."

"What? That's... that's impossible, right?"

Jeremy chewed on his lip. He seemed to be thinking a few steps ahead of me, like he'd already processed the news. "Malaki says Smith Dawes started the shop fire. Says Allison is might be dead. He mentioned the runoff streams by the hills. It's a... a mess."

It was like something heavy pierced my chest and twisted. Smith Dawes was the one behind all this? Malaki escaped? What the hell was going on and how would I explain all this to Naomi?

He went on. "The cops are searching those hills. They'll search the house, at some point. No sign of her body yet, but... I mean, nobody's seen her in a few days. And if anyone would know, it's Malaki, so..."

"I mean, that's awful, Jeremy." I wiped at my forehead, felt the hot sun beating down on us. There was no shade on a day like this. "Isn't he a suspect?"

"Sure, he is. But they're looking into Smith Dawes, first. Malaki's been told not to leave town, but that's it for now."

I frowned. "Looking into Smith how?"

Jeremy cleared his throat and let out a heavy sigh. "Well, that's why I wanted to talk. The sheriff..."

I waited for him to say it. I knew what was coming.

"He's gone to arrest Anne Dawes and Smith. Both. Wants to keep them in custody, forty-eight hours, see if he can dig up anything else. I'm sure he'll... question 'em." Jeremy ran a hand over his face. The man looked exhausted and beaten. "Some of the church women are watching the other two kids for a few days. While it's all sorted out."

I felt something rising in me. It was like anger but mixed with fear. How could I explain *this* to my wife? And our kids? It didn't make any sense. It was wrong. I hadn't decided if the Dawes were innocent or not, but trusting Malaki *definitely* felt wrong. If he was being honest, why hadn't they found Allison's body yet? Why didn't he save her, too? The whole situation didn't feel right, like there was a lot more to the story.

But Sheriff Wheeler, that man didn't care. He was out for blood. And we were all helpless to stop it.

"But how?" I ran a hand through my hair and stared at the ground. "How can he do that? What evidence is there?"

Jeremy shook his head. "Just Malaki's confession, really. The sheriff's got nothing substantial. Unless he finds more, he'll have to let them both out after forty-eight hours. But he's... just going after the easiest target right now."

"But they can't have done it!"

"Wheeler says Smith and Malaki had an incident a week ago. Says it makes sense. And I know there's been rumors about the kid —"

"Oh, so *rumors* is all it takes now?"

Jeremy threw up his hands. "Hey, I'm just telling you what the sheriff's said. I think you're right. No way they done it. But without proof otherwise, it's gonna be a long two days for the Dawes family."

"They were at the baseball game that day," I cut in, pleading with him. "We saw them! Remember?"

Jeremy's face was unchanged and his eyelids drooped. He gestured at the baseball field and walked slowly in that direction.

I fell in step beside him. "The town's in a real panic, and he's trying to save face, I think. 'Cause he's got no leads. You know how he gets. He's saying the Dawes could've started the fire before the game. Bunch of bullshit. But like I said, it's enough to hold them for now."

"There's no way. Malaki's lying."

"If he is, then it'll come out. The truth always does."

I huffed and didn't respond. *Not always.*

"I still say it's cult activity, up at the house. The missing animals, the fire, it makes sense." Jeremy lowered his voice and looked around. "I think — *if* he's lying — that Malaki knew exactly what to say. There's gotta be something else going on with all this."

I nodded. "Yeah, it doesn't feel right."

We reached the end of the alleyway, where it connected with the gravel lot. There were more cars now, and the bleachers looked nearly full. Maybe the whole town really was out here. Cheers and murmurs drifted from the crowd in waves. The smell of hotdogs and popcorn and concession food mingled with dirty gloves and sweat. And the sheriff had used this time, this distraction, to make his big move.

"Jeremy, my daughter..." I stopped walking and turned to face him solemnly. We were standing at the mouth of the alley. I almost didn't tell him. But I figured I could trust Jeremy, *needed* to trust him. "She got a text from Allison. Three days ago."

His eyebrows shot up. "What?"

"Yeah... it just makes me think... This whole situation. I don't... I don't know what happened to Malaki, but I think Allison's still out there somewhere. And he's not telling the truth."

Jeremy nodded, mulling it over. His eyes drifted to the

baseball field yet again. Or maybe to the crowd. "It's possible. It's... I agree, something's not right with his story. And the sheriff isn't gonna change his tune anytime soon. You know what I mean?"

"So, let's figure it out ourselves," I said. "You said he mentioned the runoff streams? Maybe there's answers there."

"Hmm." Jeremy kicked at the gravel underfoot. "Okay. I'm headin' to the police station right now. I gotta get the sheriff calmed down if I can. But in a day or two? You wanna head down there?"

"Yeah." I pressed a hand to my head. "Damn, this isn't good."

"No, it sure isn't."

"I've gotta get back to the game, but I'll... Just keep in touch, okay?"

Jeremy nodded and offered a hint of a smile. "You know I will."

I said a quick goodbye and headed toward the bleachers. With a miserable sun overhead and a terrible weight on my back, I tried to figure out how I would break the news. How much the kids needed to know and what I would only reveal to Naomi.

Tragedy at the baseball game. I lowered my head and approached the cheering, oblivious spectators.

CHAPTER 8
NAOMI WOODS

When he finally showed up, Cliff was red-faced and sweaty. Kaia and I scooted to the left to make room for him. We had to really cram together, because the bleachers were totally packed. That away team must've brought a lot of parents and fans.

"What was that about?" I asked as he sat down.

Cliff's eyes drifted past me to our daughter, who was intently watching the game. He shook his head, a tiny movement.

"What?"

"I'll tell you later," he said, voice low. I could barely hear him over the crowd. "Not good."

We watched the last four innings of the baseball game in silence. Cliff's eyes were glazed over, like he wasn't really watching. I couldn't help my mind from racing, imagining the worst possible scenarios. I was dying to know what he'd found out. And why he needed to wait to tell me.

I barely noticed when the ninth inning arrived and the game was tight. Nate's team pulled out a victory: a close-call, two-run win. Kaia cheered and waved her arms. I tried to put on a smile, but she probably saw right through it. Both me and Cliff stiff like boards, as the crowd celebrated.

Thankfully, that exuberant crowd started to disperse. The players shook hands and returned to their dugouts. The sun continued to pound us, relentless. But I barely noticed any of it.

"I'll go get Nate, I guess," Kaia offered, casting us both questioning looks. Then she hopped down the bleachers, stepping around people, and made her way toward the dugout.

"So?" I turned to Cliff, unable to wait any longer. "What is it?"

He let out a deep breath he'd been holding and shook his head. "Malaki's back."

"*What?*"

"Yeah. Showed up at the police station today with... some story."

"Oh my God." I stared at him, unblinking. "What'd he say? Where's Allison?" Something had shifted in my chest. I knew this was just the beginning.

He buried his face in his hands for a moment, dripping sweat into the sizzling bleachers. "Jeremy wasn't super specific. Said Malaki was at the house. With Allison. Someone... took them both captive. And Malaki escaped."

"Allison?"

"He didn't say." Cliff sat upright and stared into the distance. Toward the house, perched on the line of hills, like a watchtower.

"So... so Malaki said someone..." I noticed Cliff flinch. He still hadn't met my gaze. "Who?"

Through clenched teeth, "Malaki said it was Smith Dawes. He also said... that Smith burned down George's shop."

"No. No, he..."

Cliff turned to face me. He looked defeated and—very succinctly—nodded. Then his eyes shifted away from me, over the crowd below us. I followed his gaze, saw Kaia collecting Nate by the dugout, the rest of the baseball players merging with their families. The whole crowd would soon move toward the parking lot, leaving this field empty.

"What do we tell Kaia?" he asked.

I paused. It was my turn to avoid eye contact.

"Naomi?"

"What did the sheriff do after Malaki's story?"

Cliff hesitated. It was like a hand gripped my throat. I stood from my bleacher seat and stared down at him. Barely managed to squeak, "Tell me, Ben."

"He went to arrest Anne Dawes and her son. For Malaki, Allison. The fire. All of it."

I turned and descended the bleachers. I moved from one to the other, nearly tumbling down. A red haze clouded the corners of my vision. A red heat melted against my skin, and I felt a fire inside me, unquenchable flames.

"Naomi, wait—"

"No!" I wheeled around, halfway down the bleachers, and glared at him. "No, I will *not* wait. Come on, Cliff! We need to go."

I spun away from him and dashed off the bleachers. Through the thinning crowd, I saw Kaia and Nathaniel. I motioned them over quickly and then marched toward the parking lot.

My family followed, as I shoved my way through clusters of folks, no apologies. My feet crunching on gravel, I basically floated to the truck. I didn't feel any of the steps I took. Instead, I stormed my way to the passenger side and then turned abruptly to watch the other three draw closer.

Cliff and the kids navigated to me. His expression was unreadable, except for the shame there. The kids were engrossed in their own conversation, probably about the game. But I could only think about one thing. Sheriff Wheeler and how I could make his life a living hell. I needed to gather the other women from church, the ones who'd known Anne, *truly* known her. We needed a plan.

The men had screwed this up by not acting soon enough, by not standing up for the Dawes. They were stuck in the "old boys club." It was time for us, the women, to take matters into our own hands. We were always the ones to get things done. Now we'd have to again.

"Naomi…" Cliff hurried to my side while the kids chatted their way to the back of the truck.

Nathaniel threw his baseball gear into the bed and then climbed in himself. Kaia made the same decision and hauled herself up and over. But Cliff lowered his head and tried to whisper with me, right by the passenger's side.

"How do we tell—"

"Like this." I marched over beside the truck bed and stared each of my children right in their faces. I sensed Cliff beside me, trying to pull me back. My eyes lingered on Kaia, and I tried to soften my tone, but that red haze still gathered around my vision. "Listen… something's happened."

Nathaniel's eyebrows rose, but Kaia turned fully to look at me. Her lips quivered, like she suspected it.

"Malaki came back. Alone." I cleared my throat and cast my eyes upward, to the sky, where no comfort waited. "He told a lie. And the sheriff has gone to arrest Ms. Dawes and Smith."

"No!" Kaia exclaimed. She tried to stand up, but I put a hand on her shoulder. "What about Allison?"

"We don't know." I shook my head gravely, watching them both. "Malaki is a liar. So we don't know where she is. I'm goin' to the police station. I need you two to go home with your father—"

"Mom," Kaia interrupted, "the sheriff can't just do that! She's still—"

Cliff stepped beside me and offered, "The sheriff has—"

"No! She's not—!"

"Kaia." I gripped her shoulder, taking deep breaths. "Nathaniel." I glanced at him, too. "Listen to me. Don't *ever* let someone walk over you, or walk over someone else, because they have power. Power doesn't mean shit."

I felt Cliff tense beside me, but I didn't care at this point.

"Why would he do this to them?" Nathaniel asked quietly. "Smith isn't... he's nice..."

"That sheriff, going after their family? He's a coward, okay? And I won't let him do it. But I need you two" —I cupped Kaia's face in my hand as she started to tear up— "to go with your father. It's all gonna be okay. I'll talk to the sheriff. I'll get him to go check the abandoned house for Allison."

Cliff moved around to the driver's side while I tried to calm our kids. Nathaniel was shaken more than anything, but Kaia looked furious and terrified. I felt the same way. I saw myself in her. It hurt, more than ever, knowing I couldn't heal some wounds. And if anything did happen to her best friend, I wouldn't know what to say.

Those tearful eyes gazed up at me, desperate for answers, for an okay world. And I couldn't make it okay.

When I finally climbed in the passenger's side, I found Cliff watching me uncertainly.

"Can you drop me off at the station?" I asked him, leaning my head back. I felt a horrible headache coming on any minute.

"Naomi... Do you want me to go with you?"

"No. Just take the kids home. I—*we*—can handle this." I hesitated. "Sorry, Ben, but you boys need to let us handle this."

He sighed. "Fine. You're right."

"Just drop me off please?"

"Naomi..."

I closed my eyes so I didn't have to see his expression.

"Are you... you're sure the Dawes aren't involved? That Malaki is actually lying?"

I could've exploded right then. I turned slowly to face him. My whole vision had gone red now.

"This is *why* I have to fix things. 'Cause you're too scared to take a stand." I kept my voice low, hoping the kids wouldn't hear. I knew they were trying to listen. "You're supposed to be on my side, Ben."

"I am, hun, I just... Don't you think the sheriff has a reason —?"

Throwing open the door, I stepped out of the car before he could try to stop me.

"Naomi, wait —"

"Of *course* you'd stick with your old pal," I snapped, slamming the door in his face. "You always do!"

Cliff groaned as he climbed out of his seat. He addressed me from across the vehicle. A good thing, too, because I could've slapped him.

"I'm sorry, I just —"

"You *always* stick with them. The old boys' club, huh? After what I *told* you about the sheriff, after what you've *seen* him do?" I crossed my arms and spat vehemently on the ground. "I can't believe you, Ben. Damn it, just *trust me* for once! Fine, I'll do it all by myself. With people who *want* to help. Let us women deal with this."

He babbled some sort of apology, but I didn't listen. I reached for both of my children and pulled them closer, gave them a kiss on the forehead.

"You two stick together, okay? No matter what."

They nodded, both tearing up. I knew I shouldn't have yelled in front of them, but some things are too important to say quietly. I expected I'd do a lot of yelling before the day ended. So I marched off, toward Main Street, and thought about which of the church women I needed to dial first. Probably Susan.

Cliff, cowering on his side of the truck, called out, "Be careful, please."

I whipped around to face him one last time. "The time to be careful was days ago. It's time to do something."

CHAPTER 9
BENJAMIN "CLIFF" WOODS

I knew it was the wrong thing to say as soon as I said it. And I didn't blame Naomi for storming off like that, because I was clearly in the wrong. Playing devil's advocate was one thing, but not for someone like Sherriff Wheeler. She was right. I knew he'd gone after the Dawes with no evidence. I knew they were most likely innocent, and even if not, he had no right to hunt them down like that.

I'd even sided with him. In small ways but meaningful ones. I'd gone along with it. I'd let it happen. I was as much to blame as anyone else in New Haven. The backward locals who I thought I was so different from.

Turns out, I wasn't any better.

I stood by the driver's side door, frowning at my kids. The parking lot had emptied around us. Just my truck and a whole lot of barren gravel. Kaia and Nathaniel were staring at me like they thought I might have answers. I had nothing.

Nate spoke up first. "What's she gonna do, Dad?"

"Why don't you two sit up here?" I said, gesturing at the empty seats. "I'll... try to answer your questions on the way home. But I don't know much." *Clearly you know nothing.*

They climbed out of the truck bed while I took my spot behind the wheel and started the engine. It roared to life as Nathaniel opened the passenger door and sidled into the middle seat. Kaia took up her spot by the window, staring into the distance. I couldn't even guess what she was going through right now. The news must've hit her the worst.

I made a slow turn in the gravel and headed for Main Street. There weren't many people in sight. No Naomi. A few stragglers from the baseball game standing outside the sports bar and grill, and a few others down by the diner. But the town wasn't teeming with life. The out-of-towners had made a quick exit, and everyone else crept back into their homes.

"Where's Mom going?" Nate asked again.

"Police station," I answered uncertainly. "She's... I think she'll get some of the women from her church group and try to make Sherriff Wheeler... well, I don't know. They'll try something."

We turned onto Main Street, past the small group outside the restaurant. I glanced to the left, in the direction of the police station, but didn't see Naomi anywhere. There were very few people in sight. Pedestrians, their heads bowed, shuffling under the sun's merciless glare. Nobody had much purpose in town on a hot day like this. I knew the sheriff had been waiting for his chance. When everyone cooked at the ball game and returned home, they were exhausted and sweaty. He'd always been the scheming kind.

"I'm worried about Allison," Kaia blurted out. I didn't look over, but it sounded like she was fighting back tears.

"I know, honey." I shook my head, so helpless. My truck trudged along Main Street and the lifeless sidewalks of New Haven. "I... I don't think anyone knows where she's at."

"Malaki does. But the sheriff doesn't even care," she

snapped. "He's too worried about... about punishing someone."

"You're right," I offered. "He's not doing his job."

Nate opened his mouth but shut it again. He peered ahead, lost in thought.

"I know she's not dead." Kaia hugged herself and stared at the floorboards. "I know it." She looked over at me. "What did Malaki say about her?"

"He said they were at the abandoned house and only he escaped. But he was probably lying about all of it, Kaia."

Kaia chewed on a thought.

"It doesn't mean much," I added. "He could've... He's probably making up the whole thing. Allison could be anywhere."

"Yeah." She groaned. "I... I've just got this awful feeling. Like maybe... maybe he was keeping her locked up somewhere. And she escaped and he just wants *his* story out there first."

"Wouldn't she come back to town, then?" Nate asked.

"I mean... yeah." Kaia swallowed hard. "Maybe she's trying. Maybe she's injured."

"Or maybe they got lost," Nate suggested.

The two of them went on, spinning wild theories for most of the ride home. I didn't care to comment. My imagination had grown old and weary. It didn't make sense for me to speculate, but I understood why they did. Kaia had a lot invested in this. Her best friend. Her lies to the sheriff. And Naomi, how she wanted to protect the Dawes... Even Nathaniel had a friend involved; Smith, from baseball.

They were all drawn into this mess. And I sat beside them, just a taxi driver, taking them to town and back.

Obsolete. I tried to shake the thought away, but it returned. *Unnecessary. Unneeded.*

I was supposed to protect my family, and yet here they were, diving head-first into a dangerous situation. The most dangerous thing any of us had ever seen in New Haven.

I wanted to protect them, but I felt like they were swimming away from shore and I was too tired to chase after. Too afraid of deep water. Too willing to sit by, idle, pointless.

I'd been sitting by as the sheriff hunted innocent people. And now, as my family drowned?

The winding road led us past Jeremy's house, his sprawling fields. He was probably at the police station right now, trying to help my wife. He always sprang into action. Like when the fire started, he took off running. And I sat, pointless. I was never the first to help. Never one to dive in. Too afraid of deep water.

Dark, looming, the foreboding house waited in the background beyond Jeremy's. Sitting in the hills. The same hills where rainfall collected, people disappeared, and secrets went to die.

Maybe Jeremy had been right.

I turned into the long driveway of my own home and breathed a sigh of relief. I always felt safer here. A safety that I'd created. I'd built this home, this farm, from nothing. I wasn't pointless, then. But something in the back of my mind persisted and clawed at my skull.

"What if…" Kaia paused as we rumbled over the gravel. "Maybe she's trying to send me a message."

The truck shook from side to side, my teeth chattering against each other. I waited a moment, deciding what I'd say. I didn't want to dash her hopes, but I didn't want her making any reckless choices either.

Kaia opened her phone and stared at it, unblinking. Reading those text bubbles for the hundredth time. We pulled in front of the barn and I shifted into park. Nobody moved.

you were right.

i really messed up

i'm so sorry for everything

"Kaia…" I clenched my jaw, staring straight ahead at the red barn doors.

She glanced over at me, pocketing her phone. "What?"

"You could try to ask her a question," I suggested. "On your phone. But… but don't do anything irrational, okay? Don't try to meet her or anything. I don't want you getting hurt."

Kaia raised her eyebrows. "It's a *text,* Dad. And why not? I wanna help her, even if—"

"You don't know, one-hundred percent, that it's her, Kaia." I fought to keep my voice leveled 'cause I didn't want to come off as angry or frustrated. "Just… someone could've taken her phone, you know? It might not… really be her."

"Whatever." She forced open the door and started to climb out of the car.

"Kaia, listen—"

"No, Dad." She spun around, her eyes rolling back. "I can't wait and see if my best friend turns up or not. Or if she's *dead.* I actually wanna help. I'm not like you."

She stormed off toward the house before I could get in another word.

I watched as she marched onto the porch and in the door. She slammed it behind her so loudly I could hear it from the truck. Nathaniel, who'd been watching her too, turned to me with a frown.

"Let's head inside," I said. I opened my own door and groaned as I stepped out.

Nathaniel hurried around to the truck bed and grabbed his baseball gear. He slung the heavy sack over his shoulders and struggled toward the house. I trudged beside him, not willing to look up from the ground.

I didn't feel angry at Kaia, just like I didn't feel angry at Naomi. Simply confused and lost. Uncertain of my role in this mess. How could you warn someone without pissing them off? I didn't want my family to get hurt, but it seemed like I was pushing them away.

"At least you won, right?" I tried to laugh, but it came out hoarse.

Nathaniel stopped when we reached the porch. He left his bag on the bench swing and turned to face me.

"You never practiced with me, Dad."

Standing by the door, my hand on the knob, I felt a rush of guilt. Enough to turn my legs into jelly.

"I… I'm sorry, Nate. It's been…"

"It's fine. At least I won."

His expression wasn't even sad, and that's what hit me the most. He frowned at me, but his features were more passive than anything. Apathetic. Like he didn't care anymore.

"No, it's not fine." I took a deep breath, shaking my head. "I shouldn't make excuses. Let's practice this week, okay?"

"If you say so." Nate looked at the door, waiting for me to open it. He didn't make eye contact.

"How about we get some ice cream tonight to celebrate the win?" I suggested. "And that way, you know I mean it. I'm done making excuses." I couldn't help Naomi right then, but I could repair this relationship at least. While she faced the sheriff without me.

Nate smirked and nodded his head quickly. "Okay, sure. But can we go inside now? It's so hot out here."

"Sure thing." I pushed open the door and stepped into the cool, airconditioned kitchen. "Let's leave in an hour, okay?"

CHAPTER 10
KAIA WOODS

When I went inside, the very first thing I did was text Allison.

where are you, ally?

I didn't expect an answer. It was a shot in the dark, really. But I was going to take my shot, one way or another. I was going to help.

Only a few minutes later, my phone dinged.

the house

My heart skipped a beat. I fell backward on my bed, holding the screen in front of my face. I almost couldn't believe it. I didn't want to. But it made sense. It felt right.

i'm coming, ally

Nate knocked on my door only minutes later. When I opened it, I found him shifting on his feet, unable to meet my eyes.

"Nate? What's wrong?"

He sniffled. "I... Kaia, I know what happened to Malaki."

I frowned, leaning against the door frame. "What do you mean?"

He gulped, staring up at me with a terrified expression. "He did go to that house. I heard about it. But I didn't wanna tell you. Mom told me not to."

"She *what?*"

"And now Dad's taking me to get ice cream soon, and I..." He breathed out, raspy. "I thought you should know. I don't know what you're planning."

I pulled him against me, hugging him tightly. Nate put his arms around me too and hugged back. He almost never did that. I squeezed him, kissed his sweat-coated forehead. And then let him pull away.

"Thank you for telling me, Nate."

"I know how much she means to you." He bit his lip, hard enough to draw blood. "Please be careful, Kaia. I love you."

"I love you too, Nate. Don't worry about me." I clasped him on both shoulders, smiling wide. I didn't feel happy, but I smiled bigger than I had in days. I wanted him to know how much I appreciated this. How much *he* meant to me.

When Nate had gone, I started preparing. I grabbed my shoes, a flashlight, the small container of pepper spray Mom had bought me two years ago. I also grabbed the clear quartz necklace from my dresser. The one meant for someone else.

It hurt me to put the string over my head, let it fall beneath my shirt. But I wanted to wear it. If I actually found Allison, I'd give her this necklace right away. I'd give her everything.

i'm coming, ally

If Mom convinced the sheriff to go check it out — and I had a feeling she would — then it wouldn't hurt to go myself. They could save me, if I needed saving. And if I found Allison first, I'd be the hero. Her hero. I would keep texting her. I would use my flashlight, all the courage in my body, and I'd make it work.

My mom would probably be mad. But I knew, if I succeeded, she'd also be proud. This was something she never could do. And I was gonna do it.

Less than an hour later, Dad and Nate were standing by the front door. I lounged on the couch, trying not to appear suspicious. The two of them were about to leave. I exchanged a look with Nate. He seemed worried.

"Want me to bring you anything?" Dad called from the door.

"Nah." I tried to steady my voice, because I heard it shaking. "I'm gonna sleep soon."

"Alright. See ya in a bit," Dad called as he exited the house. "Call me if you need anything." He closed the door behind him.

Sitting alone, I didn't speak. I wasn't sure I could've. My tongue was glued to the top of my mouth, hands shaking wildly, legs bouncing up and down. After I grabbed the keys to my mom's green Chevy Malibu, I sat down on the couch again, staring at a blank television screen. Building up the courage for what I had to do, what Allison needed me to do. I touched the stone resting against my bare skin and shivered.

In my mind, I could see the route. Everybody knew how to get to that house. How to find the country road which ran along the hills. It seemed like nobody else had dared to search the house yet. They would put it off, avoid the inevitable. Nobody else had the guts to do what I would, or the desperation. But I had plenty of both.

Allison needed me to rescue her. Malaki's story had been some kind of warning. I knew it. A warning that, if I didn't act fast, her body *would* turn up, and I'd lose her forever.

I didn't trust the sheriff to find her, if he even went to look. Only I could do it. Mom was taking matters into her own hands. It was time for me to do the same.

Through those cursed hills. Past the tangled weeds and jutting-out overlooks. It felt like such a long distance. For about ten minutes, I waited on that couch, just to be sure Dad wouldn't come back for a forgotten wallet or anything. If he came back and saw my mom's car gone, burst into the house, called with no response... Well, I knew he'd know.

It just made sense. It was the place that held answers, to everything, and I was determined to seize them from its clammy, dead hands.

The house on the hill watched me. It observed without a sound as I exited the front door. My steps were short, unsteady. A cloud hung over me, persistent anxiety. A single thought tugged at my mind, threatened to untie all of my courage. As my feet left the safety of the deck, I glanced back over my shoulder, at the home I'd always known. And maybe I would never know it again.

Behind that watchful house, the sky darkened, from a pink-yellow to a deep, unsettling purple. The clouds were passing spectators, and none of them stuck around to watch. Without a second thought, I drove my mom's car away from our house and toward that heavy shadow. It became harder and harder to see as the sun disappeared, but I knew the way by heart. We all did in New Haven. We'd grown up under its glare and would always know how to find it.

It was something I'd dreamed of, had nightmares of, sometimes at the same time. A portal into another world, in a way. The building that would never give up its secrets without a fight. I had fight in me, I had persistence. I would pester the inside of that abandoned house, tear it apart, until it gave me the truth.

Allison depended on me. Maybe the whole town did.

<><><>

And then I stood on the front porch. My back to the town of New Haven.

Mom's car sat on a slab of cracked concrete with grass growing around it. There was a fountain beside the house. The ceramic base, coated entirely in mold. Vines growing on it. Like it hadn't been used for a hundred years. I could only imagine the inside of the house. Just as forgotten. Just as unsettling.

I was tiny compared to this hulking structure. I'd underestimated the size of the house, quite frankly. I didn't realize how many floors there were, how many rooms. Places to hide. Places to be hidden. I started to have second thoughts, standing on rotten wood that might cave in at any moment. A part of me wanted to look down, peer between the slits, and another part wanted to turn back.

I overruled them both. I grasped the door handle and shuddered at its icy touch. Then I twisted. An awful, creaking sound, worse than nails on a chalkboard. The door opened without hesitation, as if it had been waiting for me. The darkness overwhelmed me and I had to take another deep breath. I had to find my deepest courage.

Think about Allison. Only her.

Not the way this house stuck out against the sky, cutting the clouds with sharp rooftops and staring at me with empty glass. Not the way all light seemed to avoid it, how the interior lacked any life or hope or anything but death. Not the way this house strangled everything and would strangle me if I let it.

It was for everyone else that I stepped forward. I had no reason to come here. I had no questions myself. But I did have a friend who had gone missing. I knew the family in town under attack.

Just do it, I cursed myself. *Just do it. You're not a coward.*

For New Haven and answers. For a better future and a brighter sun when I came back out, if I ever came back out.

I took my first step into that abyss. My pale flashlight directing me. And I heard what sounded like a little girl crying from up above me. All around me an empty, spacious room, silhouettes in every direction, maybe objects or maybe humans, it didn't really matter. This place could swallow me at any moment.

There was a sense of being drawn in. The door shut behind me, and I couldn't remember if I'd pushed it. But now everything was darkness, and it touched me, it caressed my legs and shoulders. I shivered, taking another step, and then another, hoping somebody might pull me out.

But there was, of course, nobody. I was the one here to save, not to be saved. Even if they came, it might be too late.

The meager beam of my flashlight drifted over the empty space. I saw a staircase, rotten, unsturdy.

It could eat me at any second. I had the realization that I was powerless, that I was at the mercy of an unseen force. A force that wanted to grab me and pull me into that darkness.

It was impossible to not be afraid. Maybe I should've tried harder. Maybe it would've gone differently in the end.

But as I stood there, hugging myself, unable to see my own nose, I knew I had to be afraid. I knew I had to give up hope. To search the house, I needed to give in fully. Give up myself. For Allison.

What a funny thing to lose hope. What a relief.

I think I have to let it take me.

CHAPTER 11
BENJAMIN "CLIFF" WOODS

When it happened, I had Nathaniel with me, in my truck, cruising back to the house. We'd driven over to the interstate, where they had a Dairy Queen by the exit, and spent about twenty minutes at one of those outdoor tables. He demolished a hot fudge sundae while I ate a few chicken strips and slurped on a milkshake.

We didn't talk much. It was probably the stupidest apology, but it was all I could think of. There's no way to go back in time and practice with your kid. There's just trying to do better, trying to set aside time for him, for the whole damn family. I hadn't been doing a good job of that. Not since the fire at George's shop, but not ever, really.

I texted Naomi twice while we were at that table, offering an apology to her too, and promising I'd support her if we really did this. Really went head-to-head with Sheriff Wheeler.

When she finally responded, it wasn't at all what I expected.

The sheriff isn't letting Anne go tonight, but he is going to check out the abandoned house. I convinced him. I'm going up there, but no way in hell am I going inside

I texted back, feverishly. *Naomi, I'll come too. I'm at DQ but I can be there in 20 mins*

After a few minutes, she answered. *No, it's okay. I'm sorry I yelled. I just want the sheriff to go up there and make sure.*

Me and my son set off, in the pitch-black night, heading for town. I called her on the phone as we pulled out of Dairy Queen.

"Hello?" she answered. Her voice sounded worn out and strained, but it was nice to hear it again.

"It's just me." I paused. "We're heading back from DQ."

"You buy me something?" she chuckled.

"I…"

"I'm kidding." She took a deep breath. "Can you put me on speaker?"

I did and set the phone on the seat between us.

"Hey, sweetie," Naomi said. "How was the ice cream?"

"Good." Nate added quickly, "When will you be home, Mom?"

The roads leading out to the Dairy Queen didn't have any streetlights, and the sky was choked with clouds that night. Not a single beam of moonlight reached out. The rain started up too and grew harder. I turned my windshield wipers to the highest level. They were slashing angrily as my truck's pale headlights led the way home.

Naomi answered, but it was drowned out by the rain. I turned the volume up.

"What'd you say?" Nate asked.

"Not 'til late," she said. "I'm sorry, baby. It's almost your bedtime, anyway."

I expected Nate to smile at this. Instead, he peered ahead, frowning at the storm as it bashed against my truck.

"Are you okay, Nate?" I asked.

"I need to tell you something." He took a deep breath.

Naomi spoke from the phone. Her tone was deadly serious.

"Nate?"

"I told Kaia that Malaki had been going to the abandoned house," he admitted, lowering his gaze. He stared at his knees. I thought he might be on the verge of crying.

Shit. I pressed harder on the gas, the engine roaring in response.

"Naomi, I should meet you there," I spoke up.

"No, Ben. Just... just get Nate home. Keep him safe." Her voice was shaking now. "When did you tell her, Nate?"

"Earlier. Before we left."

"That's... thank you for telling me." Naomi groaned. "Ben, take me off speaker, please?"

I propped the phone on my shoulder and used both hands to steer through the downpour. The rain was violent and thundering. I sped up, sending rainwater cascading to the sides. I gritted my teeth, kept my brights on. There wasn't a car in sight and I didn't want a deer running out and surprising me.

"Naomi, I can come–"

"Ben, please just take him home." Her voice was beyond shaking now. Panic had set in. I could feel it myself, heart pounding. "I don't want all of us at that house. I... Let's... Just keep him safe."

"I want to keep *you* safe."

"I'm fine, Ben. The whole police department will be there. And Jeremy."

The lights illuminated the ghostly trees swaying in the wind and the raindrops smacking like bullets on the road. One, single car appeared ahead, so I turned my brights off.

"But what if Kaia's there?"

Naomi paused. "I'll do whatever I have to. I'll keep her safe."

"You can't go inside–"

"I don't think I'll have to. But if…"

Headlights showing only chunks of the road. I squinted in the darkness as the other car passed me. It would've been the worst moment possible for a deer to leap out. I forced myself to stay alert, foot hovering over the brakes. I had to hurry, but I didn't need a car wreck, either.

"I'm coming, Naomi."

"I'm so sorry, Mom," Nate blurted out.

"It's okay, Nate," I tried to comfort him. "You weren't trying to hurt anyone."

A road sign flew by. The rain beat even harder against my truck's hood. In total darkness, guided by dim headlights, the forest whooshing by, each tree leaning toward us. The panic grew. What if we were too late?

"I'm gonna hang up," Naomi said. "We're about to leave. Heading up there."

I tried to focus on the road, but the swirling winds made those huge maple trees bend in a way I didn't care for. If one happened to fall…

"I'll meet you there."

"Ben, please just…"

Fifteen minutes away. I was speeding along, spraying water from both sides of my truck. The roads were dark reflections of the sky. I could only see ten feet at a time. Trees whipped past. Road signs. Shadows. Large bushes. Web-like tendrils jutting out from the forest.

Then I saw him. Standing almost in the road, head bowed.

I slammed my foot on the brake. The truck skidded and my stomach lurched.

"Oh, shit. Naomi, I need to go."

He stood there, staring at the ground, with the rain beating down on him. Thoroughly drenched.

"Ben? Are you okay?"

"Yeah, just… there's a kid out here."

"What? A kid?"

"Yeah, I… I don't know. I'll call you back. I love you."

"I love you too, Ben. Please be safe."

I would've laughed at the irony–her telling *me* to be safe–if not for the situation.

"Stay here," I said to Nate. I jumped out of the truck and moved toward the dark figure.

He couldn't have been older than thirteen or fourteen. About Nate's age, then. He had on a rain-drenched sweatshirt with the hood pulled up, but I could see shaggy, brown hair spilling out as I stopped beside him. I could've kept driving. Maybe I should've. It's hard to say after everything that happened.

As sheets of rain pummeled me, I called out, raising my voice over the storm. "Hey, kid, are you okay?"

His head rose and those penetrating, green eyes settled on me. His face wasn't frightened or even confused. He was expressionless, very calm.

"Sir, may I… may I have a ride?"

"Yeah. Nate, scoot over."

I climbed back into the truck. Nate moved over hastily, pressing himself close to me. The boy moved toward the truck door and then opened it. He climbed inside, dripping all over the place, lowering his head again. I couldn't make out his face very well when he did that.

"What's your name?" I asked, frowning at him.

He pulled back his hood. Sopping wet, brown hair hung over his eyes. The sweatshirt clung to his boney arms as he hugged himself and stared into the dashboard.

"My name is Rhys."

I pulled back onto the road and rubbed the side of my head. This wasn't what I'd expected or wanted. I didn't know this kid, had never seen him in my life. But I couldn't just dump him back on the side of the road. Even though I was in a hurry. Even though I needed to be there. I couldn't just leave him. Naomi wouldn't, either.

"Do you… want me to take you somewhere?" I felt Nate squeezing himself against me, his mouth sealed. I glanced over at Rhys, who kept his eyes forward. "Do you live in New Haven?"

"I do not." He sighed. "I don't have a family yet."

Why now? The sheriff was already breathing down my back. Even if he was listening to my wife for tonight, he'd be pissed about her leading protests outside the station. And this kid, he was definitely a stranger. The definition of one. From out of town. Maybe a runaway or maybe an orphan, hell, I had no idea.

Keep to yourself. Trust nobody. That's what the sheriff said.

"Rhys…" I exhaled and tapped my fingers on the steering wheel. "So, you don't have anywhere in town to go? Nobody who you know?"

He shook his head. "Not anymore."

"Why were you out here, then?"

"I just need a place," he said, voice shrinking. "A place that's warm and dry. I thought I could find one here."

I guess he'd been right in the end.

"Alright, you can stay with us tonight," I said, trying to keep my voice stern and unwavering. "This is Nate, my son. We're heading home. After one stop."

"Thank you, sir." He looked over at me, scanning myself and then Nate. He smiled. "You won't regret it."

CHAPTER 12
KAIA WOODS

The first thing I noticed when I stepped through the front door was the staircase straight ahead. Narrow, wooden steps leading to the second floor. They looked rotten and not safe.

I moved my flashlight beam to the left and right, made out a hallway past the staircase, a vanishing act. Whatever I'd heard from up above me, what I'd thought of as a little girl crying, went silent. I stood inside the house on the hill with only a flashlight for protection, all alone, in the quiet, calm darkness.

To my right, there was an opening. The flashlight revealed a table beyond it, ornate and dusty, with cobwebs clinging to the legs. I turned to my left and saw some type of living room. Through the entrance choked with spiderwebs, there was an antique-looking chair beside a small table.

I pushed ahead, past the staircase, and found a hallway in the back of the house. It ran parallel to the back wall, with windows peering out. I stepped closer to one and looked out. I could barely make out the outlines of the forest in the distance, across a stretch of waist-high grass. There was lightning on the horizon, illuminating briefly the stark outlines of the tree canopies against the jet-black sky. And something in the underbrush, crouching. But when the light faded, it all returned to a murky, dark mass.

Using my flashlight, I worked my way through the back hallway. Many of the windows were shattered, leaving vacant holes in the wall. Wind smacked my face as I tried to walk quietly. Every noise I made was like a thunderclap in this eerie silence. Above me, the second floor creaked, an awful sound that reminded me of children screaming. Maybe that's what I'd heard when I first stepped in here.

I wasn't sure how long I moved around in that back hallway, but it felt like ages. It seemed to stretch on endlessly. As I moved further to the left, the air around me grew colder. I started to shiver, and I decided to turn around. If I needed to go down this hallway, I would, but not without checking some of the other rooms first.

I returned to the front of the house, peering around. Not nearly as cold. I was about to go into the cobweb dining room when I heard something behind me.

From the room to the left, where I'd seen the armchair, I heard somebody humming.

With my flashlight directed ahead, I stepped through the entrance, batting away spiderwebs and flies. I looked around in all directions, noticed more armchairs, large and ancient. Their surfaces were discolored and covered in dust. A strong stench met my nostrils, like centuries of hiding from the sun, mothballs, a room where the dead collected. But to my shock, I wasn't alone in the room.

She was sitting in one of those huge armchairs, right next to the fireplace, which looked like it hadn't been used in a very long time. As I turned my flashlight toward her, illuminating particles drifting through the air, I noticed she had thin, dark hair, falling around her like a mist. She wore a sheer, linen dress with a high neck. In her pale fingers, she held some kind of yellowed paper. Her hand moved on its surface, gripping what might've been a pencil. She was drawing, here in the darkness.

"Hello?" I asked, cracking the silence.

Her eyes moved lazily to me. She frowned, or perhaps she always was.

"What do you want?" She spoke in a low voice, almost a whisper.

"I'm... I'm looking for my friend." I swallowed the intense fear that threatened to strangle me. "Have you seen her?" *I will not freak out. I won't let anything here surprise me.*

"I have seen many people here." The pale woman shook her head. The linen dress shifted slightly. She continued to draw. "More than you could ever imagine."

I refused to give up. If I was going to find Allison, I needed help from somebody like her. "Can you help me, though?" I shuffled toward her, noticing the freckles on her cheeks and her lips a shade of blue.

She didn't seem to hear me. Her eyes were fixed on the drawing in front of her, half-closed, as if she was dreaming while her hand moved.

"I asked if you can help me," I repeated, slightly louder. But not too loud. I didn't want the rest of the house to hear.

I'm not afraid of ghosts, I told myself. *I'm okay in this house. I will not freak out.*

Still, the pale woman didn't respond. With a huff, I turned on her and marched back the way I'd come. If I couldn't find Allison on my own, I'd come back and ask her. But for now, I wanted to check out the back hallway again. See where it led.

Just as I stepped toward the exit which would lead me back

to the foyer, I heard her cry out.

"Wait!"

I wheeled around. My heart skipped a beat. She was standing right beside me, her face nearly pressed against mine. The pale lady's hands were stretched out, as if she wanted to grab me, but she held back. Those blue lips were wavering now. I didn't look at her feet, because I was afraid they'd be floating a few inches off the ground.

"What? Can you help me now?"

The lady paused. Her expression sent chills down my spine. Those eyes, darting around, paranoid, and her hands, in mid-air, were shaking. But I crossed my arms and tried to think brave thoughts. For Allison.

"Why are you here, child?" she asked, her voice now raspy and older. "You must get out. This is not a safe place for you."

"I *told* you, I'm looking for my friend."

"She is not here."

"I'm still gonna look."

We were speaking in whispers now. She frowned deeply and stared at me with a pitying face. "How can you expect to find her on your own?"

"I need your help —"

"I cannot help you." Her mouth continued to move, but no words came out, like she was mumbling words to herself. It disturbed me. She finally said, "I should not even talk to you. This is not safe."

"There's nobody else —"

"There *is.*"

She nodded desperately and her hand flinched toward me, like she wanted to grab mine. I didn't pull back, though it took every ounce of my courage not to. She didn't grab hold, though.

Her pale hand, floating inches away from mine.

"There is someone else and they will help you," she continued, the words hurried and jumbled. "You... you must be patient, for in time, it will arrange itself. All things will. But if you try now, you will join her and be lost forever. *Please,* be patient. She *is not* here, not where you can reach."

I gaped at her, uncertain what to answer. What did she mean 'it will arrange itself?' And why should I be patient? I'd come to do this *now*. I wanted answers *now*. But the way her lips twitched and her eyes darted behind me... It did scare me. More than anything else. And I knew I shouldn't try to find Allison alone. I knew I would need help.

Then, from deeper in the house, beyond the walls of the armchair room, I heard a growling. Like thunder, but much, much closer, just beyond the room we were standing in. There was another sound, layered under it, like the stomping of heavy feet.

The lady in front of me whimpered. She moved toward me, and I shuffled back, out of the room, back toward the house's main entrance.

"You must go, child. You must get out," she wailed, flailing her arms. "He is back from the cellar of horrors. Please, get out!"

I took a few faltering steps back, peering around the entryway. There was nobody else that I could make out with my flashlight, but still this pale lady shepherded me away. Still the horrible, deep growling emanated from deeper in the house.

"What about you?" I asked weakly. "Why don't you leave?"

"I will never again leave this house, Kaia Woods." She looked over her shoulder — the movement was unnaturally smooth, as she twisted nearly all the way around — and beckoned me toward the front door. "Not when so much has been taken from me here. You can only hope to avoid this, our fate."

And then she was gone. The growling faded. I was left in complete silence again.

Maybe that was all a test?

I took a moment to steady myself. I tried to push her image out of my mind. *I will not freak out. I won't let anything here surprise me.*

To the back hallway, then.

As I moved ahead, guided by the flashlight, I walked past the main staircase and into the back of the house. The hallway ran to the left and right. I turned left, so it would take me behind and beyond the room where I met the pale lady. To my right, the shattered windows peered out on the distant treeline. I didn't stare out there for long. I didn't know what I might see.

The floor creaked this time, which I didn't remember it doing before. Each step seemed to echo around me. I felt my legs beginning to shake. The darkness seemed to stretch on forever. Each step took me deeper into the blackness of this house.

My flashlight marked each section of wood and the strange patterns on them. Dark red splatters on some. Moldy growths on others. A smell like rotting meat, the farther I pressed on.

"Kaia?"

I froze in place. The voice came from ahead of me, but it was so dark I couldn't see. With a shaking head, I raised the flashlight and illuminate the hallway.

There were cobwebs in every corner. A long line of windows to the right, never-ending. No door or wall or any way to tell where this strange hallway ceased. But in front of me — hugging himself, shivering — stood Malaki.

"What the hell are you doing here?" I asked, taking a step forward. I kept my voice low.

"I was… I wanted to find her." He sniffled and moved closer. He shivered again, chills over his whole body. "I don't know where she is. Kaia, I don't know anymore!"

"Shh, okay. Calm down." I gestured past him. "Did you check down there?"

He nodded, sniffling again. "I thought... I thought he might've..."

"Let's go the other way, then," I said. "Go on. You first."

Malaki trudged along, leading me back the way I'd come. The two of us made a lot of noise following those creaking boards all the way toward the front of the house. I tried not to think about it.

"Why did you two come up here?" I asked him.

"Just for fun." He shuffled his feet.

"Quiet, man. Why the hell did you bring her here? Are you stupid?" I kept my eyes ahead of us, watching out for anything in the hallway. I didn't notice him fidgeting with his pockets.

He shrugged and didn't answer.

"What happened when you came here? How did you get out?"

We moved along, but I pestered him with questions, because I still didn't understand his story. I also didn't believe it. Even if he seemed terrified now, I could imagine him bringing Allison here, snarky and cruel, just to scare her. But what happened next?

"This all started when I burnt down George's shop—"

"Wait," I interrupted. "You didn't burn down his shop? You were getting married, Malaki."

He shook his head and went on, "I did it, I did it, I did it."

"Malaki, shut up. Hey. Look at me."

I tried to reach for his shirtsleeve, but he leapt forward. Malaki turned to face me. He was no longer sniffling and cowering, but instead wearing a terrible grin.

"What?" I asked.

I realized, now, that he had me cornered. Malaki was

blocking the only way out of this hallway. And I sure wasn't going to run the opposite way, deeper into the house. I needed to get past him. And get out of here.

"You didn't start that fire, Malaki."

"Does it even matter, baby?" He crossed his arms and his tone sounded like typical Malaki. Sneering. Cold. "We're both here. Alone. Does any of it even matter?"

I took a step back, listening carefully for any sounds behind me. I wouldn't let something sneak up. And I wouldn't turn my back on Malaki.

He uncrossed his arms and put them behind his back.

"Why are you actually here, Malaki?"

He shrugged and held out one hand. Holding a phone.

"'I'm coming for you, Ally.' So touching." He cackled. "Did you *really* think she was texting you? She's dead, Kaia!"

"No..." I took another step back. "No, she's not..."

"She *is*. Oh, God, she is *so* dead. I killed her, too!" That grotesque smile widened. "Just like I started the fire." He revealed his other hand now, raised it in the air. Holding a knife. "Just like I'm going to kill you."

"Malaki... Now, wait..."

Two steps back. Just enough distance.

"Oh, Kaia. I've waited so long for this moment. *So* long." He sighed. "I'll enjoy you even more than her."

"She's *not* dead!" I yelled.

And this time, I didn't back up.

I got a running start. I knew he wouldn't expect it. Malaki's eyes widened and he held the knife up, loosely, in his arm. I grabbed his arm and pummeled into his chest head-first. He toppled backward. I kicked him, hard, and clawed at his face. Anywhere I could hurt him. The knife went sliding backward and he hit the wood floorboards with a thud and a thousand creaks.

I leapt over him and dashed away, down the hallway.

"You *bitch!*" he roared. I heard him scrambling to his feet, likely grabbing the knife.

Heart pounding in my ears, I ran as fast as I could. I couldn't let him catch me. I knew he was stronger, but I was closer to the exit.

He yelled something else, but it didn't matter.

I wheeled around the corner and past the main staircase. Footsteps thundering behind me. Sweat dripping in my eyes. I reached for the door handle, gasping for air. I swung it open and toppled outside.

I was met by a thousand lights blinding me.

Red-and-blue police lights flashed in the darkness. Sirens echoed through the hills as they approached. Headlights, at least five cars, all pointing in my direction. I shielded my face and hurried away from the front door. There were shapes all around, dark figures, but I couldn't make out who or why they were.

"Kaia!" I heard a familiar voice call.

My mother.

I leapt off the porch, collapsed to the ground. I felt cool grass against my cheek. Dewdrops in my hair. I crawled away from the house, away from him.

Seconds later, Malaki burst outside, still wielding the knife, still shouting my name. The police were there, waiting. He never stood a chance.

New Haven sparkled below the hills, the streetlights and houses I'd always called my hometown. I leapt off the porch, fell in the wet grass. Rain smacked my face now. The wind had picked up, whipping against me. Familiar, warm hands reached for me, pulled me off the ground.

I heard the sheriff's voice too, shouting commands. I saw other men stalking toward the house, warily creeping onto its porch. Three of them were holding back Malaki, now wearing handcuffs. He growled quietly as they led him away from the house.

My mother's face swam into view, and I focused on it. I realized I was crying. I realized my hair and clothes and cheeks were drenched in rain. Thunder rumbled overhead, and it reminded me of the monster inside that house.

I whimpered and started to cry.

"I couldn't do it," I sobbed, burying my face in my mom's chest. "I couldn't find her."

Gut-wrenching failure. Overwhelming guilt. I sank to the ground, sitting in the wet grass as it clung to my legs. The expression on my mom's face was strange, twisted. Relief and anger mixed together. And pity.

"She's not dead!" I yelled to nobody in particular. "He... he's lying. He said he did it, but he didn't. He couldn't! Allison's *not dead!*"

It would be my fault if they couldn't find her now. I needed answers. I needed someone who could help.

But for the moment, I cowered in the grass, more drenched with each second.

Behind me, the house on the hill was silent. Holding its breath as the policemen combed it. I already knew they wouldn't find anything. No ghosts, no bodies, no clues.

They led Malaki away in a patrol car. New Haven's proudest son. Why had he lied?

"He said he started the fire, but he didn't. He was at the wedding. He didn't do that. He didn't kill Allison. He... he..."

I let the thought fade away. I didn't know what Malaki had

done. What his intentions were. Or where Allison was now.

"It's okay, Kaia." Mom rubbed my back, peering at the house herself, watching those flashlights crawl through the darkness like tiny orbs. "It's gonna be okay."

"It's not, Mom." I shook my head, choking on the tears. "I love her. And now she's gone. I failed. I failed her."

New Haven twinkled below us. The sight, to me, seemed dim. The red-and-blue police lights were a disco ball on the hilltop. I couldn't bear to look as they searched the house. I knew they could never find Allison.

Only I could. And I had failed.

ACKNOWLEDGEMENTS

One down, two go.

This novel is the beginning of my first-ever series of psychological thrillers, and I'm super excited to take you on this journey. But this novel wouldn't have been possible without the help of some important people.

My dad is always my first reader, and he gave me incredible feedback. Afterward, I got some help from fellow authors, such as Evan Myers who writes incredible thrillers and is an English teacher, too. Next, Theresa Jacobs gave some plot development tips, and Jordon Greene helped in a plethora of ways, including formatting this book.

Aspire Book Covers created the perfect cover for this book and they are already working on the covers for the rest of this series. Marni Macrae worked with me to professionally edit the book and improved it many times over. Without her, this book wouldn't have been the same.

I had family and friends who served as beta-readers and inspiration. I mentioned my mom, my grandma, and my wife in the dedication, but all of them gave this book life without knowing it and inspired me to write about one family, sticking together, in the face of everything. They embody the tenacity, hopefulness, and values that I admire and look up to.

While I hope this book entertained you, the next two are going to take things up another notch. I have so many scenes in mind, twists and turns, a shocking ending... I can't wait to show you all of it. This is far from the end.

Thank you to everybody who has made this possible, to everybody who continues to help, and finally to everybody who opened this book and gave it a chance. Without all of you, none of this would be possible. There will be more soon.

ABOUT DAVID KUMMER

David Kummer is a young author who grew up in Madison, a small, southern Indiana rivertown. He grew up in a large household with many siblings and studied English and Education at Hanover College. David is now a high-school English teacher, happily married, and living in New Albany, where he is constantly influenced by the city around him. When not writing, he enjoys listening to indie rock and watching sports, but mostly spending time with family and friends.

VISIT DAVID ONLINE AT

www.DavidKummer.com